On Submission

On Submission

Cover by Joel Amat Güell
ISBN: 9781960988812 (paperback)

CLASH Books
Troy, NY
clashbooks.com
Distributed by Consortium

First Edition 2025
Printed in the United States of America.

Praise for Michael J. Seidlinger

"Raw and alarmingly prophetic, Michael J. Seidlinger's *The Body Harvest* is a crucible of torment that lures the reader into a consecrated baptism of human suffering and then traps you there until you turn the final page and find yourself forever marked, eternally polluted."

— Eric LaRocca, author of *Things Have Gotten Worse Since We Last Spoke*

"Viscerally and metaphysically repulsive—and a dangerously accurate snapshot of a society, as only Michael Seidlinger could do."

— Stephen Graham Jones, New York Times bestselling author of the Indian Lake Trilogy

"Human connection as drug, fame as disease: Seidlinger carves from our Age of Illness a brilliantly nihilistic nightmare."

— Daniel Kraus, author of *Whalefall*

"Do not, under any circumstance, read when you're alone. One of the most disturbing novels I've read in years."

— Danielle Trussoni, New York Times Book Review

"This book makes *Cabin at the End of the World* by Paul Tremblay look like a cakewalk. This is THE MOST intense psychological horror you have ever read. Seriously. It makes *Out* by Natsuo Kirino look tame."

— LIBRARY JOURNAL (*STARRED REVIEW*)

"A tortuous affair that marries psychopathy with writerly ambition, *On Submission* is a serial killer revenge fantasy set within the publishing industry's already ruthless echelons, a social satire that enacts the darkest imaginings of any author forced to endure yet another blanket rejection slip. It's gruesome, troublesome, impish, and lampoonish —a fast-paced splatter romp whose resourceful antihero shares a moral compass with Patrick Bateman. Seidlinger doesn't just bite that hand that feeds him, he devours it."

— JOE PAN, AUTHOR OF *FLORIDA PALMS*

"Sharp in all the ways that matter. If you're not afraid of gore, want a shadowy look into the world of publishing, or savor the mind of confidently deluded characters, pick up *On Submission.*"

— *INDEPENDENT BOOK REVIEW*

"Short, sharp, bizarre and brilliant, *On Submission* is a scathing autopsy of the publishing industry."

— *FANFIADDICT*

"Seidlinger vivisects a nightmare version of the publishing world, where stories require sacrifice, self-promotion needs ferocity, and the marketplace craves scandal and atrocity."

— DENNIS MAHONEY, AUTHOR OF *OUR WINTER MONSTER*

On Submission

Michael J. Seidlinger

INTRODUCTION

In April 2020, right as the pandemic started tearing apart our lives, Christoph Paul reached out to me, hoping to get on Zoom to discuss something. That *something* was an idea, a pitch for a novel involving the publishing industry and a "boogeyman." During the same meeting, I mentioned a manuscript I had finished years before, relegated to being a "drawer novel." I accepted his pitch, and he accepted mine. That manuscript became *Anybody Home*. All the while, I worked on what might meet Christoph's challenge. I failed twice, two separate books tossed into the garbage bin, set ablaze, but eventually, third time's a charm, I found the voice of the boogeyman and tapped into the good, the bad, and the ugly of the publishing industry.

The result is the book you now hold in your hands. Simply put, this book would not exist without Christoph. Eternal thanks, my friend, for the inspiration and the continued championing of my writing. Likewise, eternal thanks to Leza Cantoral, who has always been there, during the good and during the darkest of the dark, when I felt it was easier to end it all than to keep going.

Kaitlyn Kessinger for being amazing, keeping everything and everyone in check during the hellacious tedium of the publishing process.

Angela Capovani for the skilled copy-editing and running a

scalpel through some of the more gruesome scenes with a medical professional eye.

Elena Gorgevska for giving the book a deep and thorough pass, seeking out typos, continuity errors, and run-ons.

Joel Amat Güell for the stunning cover; you always manage to capture the true pulse of a book with your designs.

Writing can be a lot, sure, but the craft, the day-by-day habitual act is a blessing, a bastion where I live through experiences as they are created. The publishing industry?

Well...

Every writer faces continuous rejection and doubt, no matter how far along they are in their careers. This book is an exorcism and an examination of the writer facing the industry. I hope that it can be a balm, in some small way, to every wounded writer out there. Publishing is such a grind. Yeah, it sucks. But writing? Writing is a sanctuary. Don't forget why you started writing in the first place.

Thank **you** for reading this book.

To Christoph
who lit the spark

"Agents cannot control whether publishers are interested in a book. Agents cannot control a publishing house's internal bidding rules, including whether it prohibits its imprints from bidding against each other for a book. Nor can an agent control how a publisher values a book. Agents cannot control how much a publisher bids for a book. Agents cannot even always control the scope of rights that they can sell."

— GOVERNMENT BRIEF, DEPARTMENT OF JUSTICE (DOJ) VS. PENGUIN RANDOM HOUSE (PRH)

Part One
WORKSHOPPING

Dear Henry,

I am writing to seek representation for my 78k-word speculative novel, FRIENDS SELLING FRIENDS. It's about a friend group since grade school, coming of age during a series of pivotal cultural moments that force them to learn harsh lessons about what it means to be alive at the onset of human commodity. There's four friends, the protagonist being Alexander, shy and withdrawn, but wide-eyed and full of creativity. He wants to become an artist. His best friends, Chadwick and Matt both want to go into STEM, earning the big bucks, while his closest friend and perennial crush, Mary, hopes to leave the country "before it falls apart" and become a chef in a small town somewhere. Things are exacerbated when they face the entry tests for college, and though they all do modestly well, a new law in place prevents them from advancement: It isn't enough to make the grade on paper; people must now put a price on themselves, and every aspect both physical and psychological, and be willing to sell it to the highest bidder.

I have a bachelor's degree from the University of Florida, where I studied sociology and psychology. Though I have not published widely, I have been writing since childhood and have been a blogger for a now-defunct fan-fiction site called ClapApplause. I live as a digital nomad and have called the northeast home for the last eight months.

Thank you for your time and consideration.

Alexander Moyer

Dear Mr. Moyer,

Thank you for trusting me with your query. Though I admire your ambition, I don't feel strongly enough about the manuscript to offer representation. Publishing is a subjective business, so keep in mind that though it's a pass from me, your manuscript may be perfect for another agent.

Respectfully yours,

Henry Richmond Pendel
Senior Agent
Cooper Willis Endeavor

Chapter 1

Someone had been inside his home. This had nothing to do with strange coincidences. Facts present themselves as evidence, which are then catalogued and filed away for the case file labeled: Henry Richmond Pendel. He has lived in this Greenwich Village apartment for seven of the 12 years he has worked as a literary agent. Like the industry he reigns over, as one of its most reputable and well-known agents and tastemakers, he knows where everything is, and knows when a room thought to be safe might have been tampered with. It could be a book on a shelf slightly askew, a volume swapped or swiped, the scent of another body. Yet even as he scans his countless bookshelves and checks every corner, he can't help but think about who has been here. Even if he hasn't, it's only a matter of time.

Alexander Moyer, where are you?

A name, an email containing a query and an eventual author rejection, has become something more. Much more. Pendel has received a steady stream of emails, communications that started off as professional, yet over the last week or so, have become odder than Pendel would like to admit. The fact that Moyer has mentioned personal details, particularly the casual namedrop of the building he lives in, has caused more than a little suspicion. This could be an omen, a warning of things to come.

He has been in contact with his lawyer. The proof he has isn't much, but it's something. But there will need to be more. A restraining order was mentioned, and it only goes so far. This isn't the first time he's been under threat of a bitter author, one hurt by his rejection, yet something about this is different.

Last night he fell asleep at his desk. When he woke up, the mug that had been next to him had been moved. A tense overview of every room revealed its new location, casually "left" next to the bathroom sink. Pendel shrugs it off, maybe just too preoccupied to remember that he brought it with him into the bathroom. No big deal. It's the arrangement of his bookshelves that reveals something definite, proof of something amiss.

He notices an entire six-volume set of sci-fi classics, a gift from one of his clients, missing, a gap where they had been alphabetized among other genre offerings. He looks for them everywhere, already late to the office, a meeting likely missed.

When he checks his inbox, perhaps expecting that familiar name—Moyer—instead he sees no new emails. He should have new emails. Every time he hits refresh, there should be new queries. There might not be a lot that an agent can count on, but they can definitely count on another flurry of queries aiming to overwhelm an inbox.

How odd, he thinks.

Instead of checking the router and discovering that it has been unplugged, seeing yet another piece of evidence, clearly tampered with, he stares at the shelves. Maybe he's already letting it get to him. This private invasion, one dealt with in a manner that is so manipulative it's difficult to understand if it's real or all in his head.

"Not like Hendrix is answering my emails anyway," he says.

Could it be that there is something more to this person, perhaps more than a mere querying author, someone he had known, someone from his past? What are the chances that Pendel has mishandled some aspect of their interactions? The chances are high, part of Pendel's ironclad reputation being his cutthroat nature, complete with a temper that intimidates and often limits people's willingness to negotiate.

It's all circumstantial, he decides, and proceeds to move on with his day. Maybe some of the morning might still be salvageable. The facts, they always rise to the top.

An agent finds reason in every conversation, even if it means not getting the best deal. In those inceptive steps—shower, shave, what to wear—Pendel finds temporary solace in fantasy, a vacation, wipe the slate clean. Just leave all this stress behind for a little while. Maybe this Moyer will move on to the next agent, the next person to personalize. Nobody talks about all the stalkers that orbit a public figure. Maybe he should take matters into his own hands. Forget the lawyer and seek the help of the authorities. This is another writer who has let the worst of this industry warp their mind. It could be that Moyer thinks it's he who is preventing him from becoming a published author. Pendel, the one with absolute power. Say the word and they become a household literary name. That's something he couldn't give any client. Sure, he can set a path, but it's up to the author to prove that they have what it takes to be a bestseller.

They got to be willing to play.

To play, you have to give up something.

When he's finished showering and is about to head out, he has no time to wait for the train, so he'll have to call a car. Never mind the ride apps; Pendel prefers this car service. A relic of a different city, you still have to call them up. They pick you up in a black luxury vehicle, complete with a driver in a suit.

Pendel walks into the back room where he left his phone on a charger. That's when he sees it: the router unplugged. Once it's powered back up, a quick reset and in minutes, his apartment's internet connection is restored, his inbox comes to life.

After calling the car service, he emails his assistant.

A note-to-self that gets lost minutes after he makes it: Tell Marina what happened. Also, make sure to show your appreciation for all that she does. What would Pendel do without his tireless assistant?

He's got a voicemail. While waiting in the lobby for his driver, he goes through the messages. They're nothing at first. White noise. And then white noise becomes breath. Breath becomes heavy breathing. The heavy breathing becomes a hint of something far more malicious. Or maybe he's just expecting Moyer's call.

It's him. Pendel's imagination is so livid and overactive it might as well be fact. Jump forward to the act two climax, where he is being manipulated by a psychopathic would-be author, complete with a list of demands and a false sense of power.

The messages blend together. Some are from friends and acquaintances he has no intention of ever reciprocating. Let every bond wither away to nothing. Working so much, it's easy to do. Pendel may even prefer his aloneness. It starts to get a little difficult to know when each voicemail was left and when—except for the one. It's the one that further confirms that it's not all his imagination. It was Alexander Moyer. It could only be Alexander Moyer.

The message in plain goes something like this:

Why do you have three copies of Infinite Jest?
You know you've never read it.

Beep. It doesn't seem like much, yet it's enough to send a message. But then the car pulls up and he is Henry Richmond Pendel, renowned literary agent at Cooper Willis Endeavor, late and lately worried about his client list. You see, he's used to selling, wheeling and dealing the best possible deal for his author list. He's not used to this dry spell, nearly a month of nothing, every editor deferring just enough to remain professional yet clear enough that nobody's finished reading any submission, and nobody is keen to make any big moves anytime soon. It's alarming, a possible sign of things to come. Last time something like this happened, the trade publishing industry suffered massive layoffs and restructuring. The whole system changed, seemingly overnight. But he's Henry Richmond Pendel, and he has no reason to be concerned, given his reputation and position. Still, it's enough of a bother to let all this concern about a vengeful author get pushed, yet again, to the corners of his consciousness. Nearly forgotten, at least for now, Pendel gets in the car and is already drafting an email response to Marina, explaining his tardiness, offering a little white lie in hopes that this meeting he's over a half hour late for is not yet lost. And when he tells her to say that "I'm willing to talk about the possibility of also selling audio rights," he knows it'll buy him more time, calming the editor-in-wait down long enough for him to get to the office. And just in case, Pendel adds a little something extra:

"You can tell him, no matter what, we'll make it happen." It's the least he can do. The editor agreed to meet at the agency office. Besides, an agent is only as good as their word.

CHAPTER 2

I don't need much to get inside—this building, this apartment, his mind. Just takes a little patience, a little bit of that creativity I usually save for the page. Really, when it comes down to it, there's no difference between fact and fiction, a story told versus a story lived. A person's body of work is only as good as what remains in a person's memory. So when I start my story, I choose one of the biggest names in this business.

Henry Richmond Pendel.

A name so presumptuous you'd think his parents took one look at him at birth and knew he'd be a walking literary stereotype. He was born in Dorchester, MA, to one Harold Anderson Pendel and Margaret Catherine Pendel, both entertainment lawyers. An only child, he was raised in an upper-middle-class household, attending a private school, which must have opened doors for his subsequent undergraduate studies at NYU, followed by graduate study at Columbia. He wasn't an agent at first; rather, he took the Columbia Publishing Course because he, and I quote from an interview that he did years later, "overheard his crush talking about it with such enthusiasm that he 'just had' to follow his lead." Of course, it was effortless, his admission into the course. Though he had already earned a master's in sociology, he went the extra mile, completing the course and quickly accepting an editorial role at

Grove Press, where he acquired three future *New York Times* best-selling authors, Vernon Childress, Mallory McAllister, and J.W. Clemens. After five years at the press, he left suddenly, in a dramatic disappearance that lasted three months. He became the subject of controversy and industry-wide worry, mostly because he was there one day and suddenly... gone.

What an inspiration! I like this part of his story. Too bad it is ruined by his reemergence. How else could it be anything but a letdown? Pendel calls up McAllister, who he had become friendly with over the years as her editor and reveals that he had a little bit of a breakdown and walked away from life to go live abroad in Europe for a few months.

He is quoted in *The New York Times* story-exclusive about his disappearance: "After 12-hour days and so much pressure, years of being told that the entire press's financial future is on my shoulders, I 'just had' to get away. I couldn't breathe. Everywhere I looked, I felt like I was being watched."

Must be nice, being able to just up and leave. Pendel started at the press as associate editor, making $56k a year, and ended his tenure as a senior editor, earning $112k a year. Some people are shooting stars, destined to be the leading role of their own story.

Pendel chose not to return to Grove, instead shifting to the agent role. He spent the first three years at 505 Entertainment, an agency focused more on the film industry. He emerged as a literary agent mere weeks after leaving 505 and joining Cooper Willis Endeavor, the biggest and oldest literary agency in the country and perhaps the English-speaking world. A power move, he poached McAllister and Childress and J.W. Clemens and made them among his first clients. Big names, easy deals. Big money. Pendel's story becomes a dizzying, seemingly endless list of deals made, many of them to the biggest editors in the business, especially Hendrix de Leon, the editor who turned J.D. Church into the "king" of horror. Church is one of his clients.

Me? I'm a storyteller on the verge of a breakthrough. It's all stacking up, for once. I've always been creative. Grew up writing fan fiction, obsessed with Marvel and DC, and then it just kept going, and I was always telling stories. There was never a time when I wasn't trying to leave an impression. At some point, all the derivative and unremarkable stuff fades away and your craft, the very essence of what you're looking to create, becomes something entirely separate, entirely your own. Like, you could be living in this building, but I'm not looking to tell your story. Mine has been a long time coming.

I took a chance. The query itself workshopped like anything else, to the point of being near perfect. I sent it to Pendel on a Tuesday in March. QueryTracker said it takes at least six weeks to hear back. I heard back in 20 minutes.

Thank you for trusting me with your query. Though I admire your ambition, I don't feel strongly enough about the manuscript to offer representation. Publishing is a subjective business, so keep in mind that though it's a pass from me, your manuscript may be perfect for another agent.

Not the most imaginative of replies, especially given how much effort went into mine, but the quickness of the reply demanded more. So I gave him another reply.

If there are any changes or considerations of note, I would gladly edit and revise to better fit what you're looking for.

Just because there isn't a reply, it doesn't mean it's a dead end. Like a door opening up to a foyer or lobby, it's often unlocked. The trick is knowing which number leads to the right scene, finding it by way of a directory, maybe hitting the buzzers to see if anybody replies. It's about taking all that time and patience and refusing rejection. It's what I did.

Turns out he's on the top floor, 7B. Lives alone, which makes it easy to peruse his shelves. For someone who represents so much genre fiction, his library is severely lacking. He does have a nice six-volume set, worth $800 these days, of sci-fi classics like *Dune* and *Stranger in a Strange Land*. He won't miss them. Probably won't even notice.

There are a number of blind spots in the house. The crawl-space near his bedroom is worth noting, though just because I've gained access to it doesn't mean I'll do anything. It's too early for any of that. Really, when I finally figure it out, it makes his rejection and silence all the more understandable. Every story has its own breakthrough, and perhaps this was what I needed to finally figure out how to get his attention and, best of all, produce something wholly original.

I unplug the router, just because. Another decoy, something fun.

A quick observation while lying in his bed: I can still smell the laundry detergent. Meaning he doesn't end up in bed as often as the average human. Asleep yet again at his desk, I listen to him snore. That neck's going to be sore.

His desk here is a mess, countless pages and bound manuscripts, the predictable mess of an overworked agent. I see that both Church and McAllister have new novels in the mix. After a quick look at them, I can tell just by the first couple paragraphs that it's going to sell. If they haven't already, they'll be deals.

I make note of their contact information listed on the front pages of their manuscripts. Maybe they can blurb my big breakthrough. They'll certainly find it interesting at least.

In due time...

He drinks his coffee black. No surprise. I hold onto the mug, walking with it as I continue down the hallway and into the bathroom. It's been cleaned recently, not a single spec of mildew or grime around the tub; the shower curtain is a pattern of astrological signs. A stack of thumbed over *New Yorkers* near the toilet. On the other side, a plunger.

Setting the mug down, I reach for the latest issue of the *New Yorker*.

What stories got his attention? Which articles? Finding a page dog-eared, I see that it's a piece of nonfiction about growing up in a family that produces wine, all the while being worn away by alcoholism. An agent like Pendel would reach out to the author in this byline. I'm sure of it. Flipping to the bio, I note the author's name, Harold Brandt. He hasn't written much, but somehow got this piece into the *New Yorker*.

After the bathroom, I stop and look out the window. A nice enough view, but one that's just so unmemorable. Carry on for a minute or two before breaking free of the moment. I find myself back at the bookshelves. Wow.

How can that be?

What I said about getting inside holds true. You can see so much in a character and a person from what they accumulate. There, taking up most of a shelf: multiple copies of *Infinite Jest.* Their spines haven't been creased or cracked.

Can't just leave this unaddressed, and now I have his number too. I'll leave a message, but for now, I walk back into the office, stare at him a moment, and then take in the entire apartment, everything I've already come up with, and everything that'll come to me in the scenes yet to unfold, wash over me. I'm anxious with anticipation, but for now, this is enough.

Like Pendel, I 'just had' to set the scene. Everything else, it'll be effortless.

Pendel's body tremors, a loud snort causing him to shift his weight in his seat.

Hush now, we're just getting started.

Chapter 3

The agency has an entire wing of meeting rooms. The editor waits patiently in one of the rooms in the back, Pendel's preference because there's more privacy, the soundproofing enough to keep any industry gossip clandestine. She's new, or at least new enough, to have actively waited for Pendel's arrival when most editors would have left after 15 minutes, seeing it as a red flag. Who wants to feel unimportant, the opposite of a priority?

"Forgive me," he says, hand over his heart. "It was a nightmare at home."

He isn't wrong. Though the excuse he provides is a bold-faced lie, "Burst water valve in the bathroom, or so the super tells me."

She's courteous, offering her hand. "It's totally okay. I understand completely."

After a handshake, they are seated across from each other, the large, lacquered oak table more garish than fashionable, yet much of the agency decorum leans that way. It's about being imposing, and nestled within the hassle is the thought that anybody who happens to be a guest must feel out of place, lesser, clearly not in their pay grade.

"Well," he exhales. "So, we were talking about the Kawada manuscript, right?"

He's already eying his phone.

"Oh," she is taken aback a little, reaching for a tablet. "Actually, we were here to talk about the latest J.D. Church." She taps the screen, which illuminates her youthful face. Pendel notices her discomfort. She's still so very new to this. Must be no older than 24, a year or two tops, as an acquiring editor. He already knows what's going to happen: She will want the latest Church manuscript but will inevitably settle for the Kawada, a debut literary novel that, according to his assistant, is quite good. Maybe it'll do well. Be optimistic, sure, why not?

"Ah, well he's still writing," says Pendel. He offers his best good-natured grin. He'd love this meeting to end sooner rather than later. Really, it shouldn't even be a thing. Who meets at the agency? This editor is out of her element.

"Umm, but..." She raises her hands, "And excuse the confusion, but... I have the manuscript right here." She gazes down at the tablet and reads the title, "*The Renegades.* It's wonderful. Frankly, it's one of his best in years. I read it in a single sitting."

"How odd," Pendel says, unfazed. The way he keeps a straight face as he comes up with yet another lie: "*The Renegades* has yet to be completed. In fact, Church told me the other day that it's only a few chapters away from being complete. I'd be happy to send it to you once it's complete!"

"How can that..." The editor is completely baffled, and by now, she may be catching on to Pendel's implications. She isn't the sort of editor who is "lucky enough" or rather "trusted" to make an offer on such a large, established name as J.D. Church. He is an author who pioneered horror back when it was tossed around as a bottom-tier paperback-only genre alongside sci-fi. He accounts for 80% of Pendel's yearly income on back catalog and rights alone. And this young, ambitious editor wants to be his editor, when Hendrix de Leon has been Church's editor for a dozen books? If you asked Pendel, he'd be inclined to say that the disrespect here is by the editor on behalf of his client. To think, this young editor barely has a Publishers Marketplace footprint, and she wants to put in an offer for a J.D. Church.

"The Kawada," Pendel changes the subject, "Now that's going

to be huge. You know that kind of manuscript where it just speaks to you? You are barely two pages into reading it and you can just sense the magic?"

He waits for her reply.

The editor clears her throat, "Umm, yes. I mean, I feel that way about every book I have bought and would only ever put in an offer if that 'magic' was there."

"Good answer," Pendel grins. "That's what an agent likes to hear. So you like the Kawada, then?"

She thumbs through some documents on her tablet and then offers a tentative nod. "I do. It's quite the romance. I think it might be just about time for vampires to get another moment in the spotlight!"

It's how the editor backs down so quickly, and how Pendel uses the situation, a place of power, that makes this meeting yet another in a long-running sequence where the interpersonal and the political end up providing the through line for a book deal. The editor went all this way thinking Pendel would work with her on finding the right terms for the latest Church, and instead, he uses the situation, backed into a corner, to sell her on a book, not exactly lesser, but viewed as less when used as leverage for what should have been its own negotiation.

But Pendel knows how to get his way; furthermore, he knows how to get the best deal. They're out of the room, handshake deal, et al.

"Send me your boilerplate and we'll make it legit!"

The editor does her best to shrug off the manipulation, and it's written across her face, the thought so commonly made and implied: *If I buy this one, maybe I'll get access to Pendel's bigger clients in the future.*

Isn't that just the way?

His assistant, Marina Grace, waits for him at the doorway. Pendel doesn't stop, brushing past her into his large, messy office. "Shouldn't they have cleaned this?" A habit of sorts, he's grown used to venting through delegation, always finding some new task to assign to the custodians, the interns, and, of course, the one directly in line with his every comment and command, Marina.

She carries her agency-issued laptop, tapping away while she says what she always says, "I'll check on that."

Pendel sighs as he collapses into his chair. Didn't get a whole lot of sleep last night. He skims through his inbox, marking every query with the tag Marina had created, every query hers to consider, and every query considered, yet only a paltry few will make the weekly list offered to Pendel for his "undivided attention."

"What was her name?" He's talking about the editor.

"You're kidding, right?" Marina says, though none of this is shocking. Not anymore. Hasn't been for quite some time. "Emily Mills, the new editor at FSG. She's on fire. Every book she's acquired has put in some awesome numbers."

"Well, good for her," says Pendel, not really listening. "Have you seen anything from J.D.? He should be keeping me up to date with his current PR and book tour. I need every bit that counts to get him some extra zeroes on that book deal."

It takes only a minute for her to do a thorough search, the project management software spitting out every mention and marking involving the bestselling author.

She shakes her head, "No, not today."

"Fuck," he hisses. "Get him on the phone."

"According to the itinerary, he is en route, flight into JFK for the Brooklyn Book Fest."

"Just get him on the line," he says, showing his desperation. "This is important."

Chapter 4

Well of course it's important. When you're a VIP, a venerable public figure that can be easily spotted at the airport terminal while you venture tiredly off the tarmac, right into the throes of a crowd, you better believe it's important to have a few people on hand.

That's how I see the author. Really, if there's any author that should be made a stereotype, it would be J.D. Church. I just love (and I mean *love*) his book, *Another Way Out.* According to all the interviews he did for the book, it came from a real, very dark place. To think he was able to write about losing his mom and then his sister, only to collapse due to a stroke, all in the span of three weeks... yeah, that's the kind of nightmare fuel that captures and creates a magnum opus. Yeah, it's his best book, by far. Never mind the fact that nobody else thinks that's true. Everyone goes to *Paradise Unfound* or *The Neverland Gang*, both becoming big film adaptations and cultural moments, or maybe they namedrop *Them*, the alien home invasion book, or maybe they cite Church being a major influence for their own writing with *Sunday Mass*, his craft/master-class on writing; or maybe they talk about *Heather Must Die*, the heinous and controversial book about a woman that becomes obsessed with removing her skin; or maybe it's really the one that everyone calls one of the best films of all time, never mind that it was a book first. Yeah. That one. *The Last Mile: A Redemption Story.* That's the one that has so many people queued up and calling out his name as he walks the terminal, hand in hand with two men who must be bodyguards for rockstars when not on Church's payroll.

Why any of these fans think they can get at him now is beyond me. Can they just take a breath and realize that maybe trying to get an autograph at the airport isn't the smoothest move?

Me, I'm kicking it safely from the center aisle of seats, watching Church do as he's done presumably many times, walking a quick enough pace, head somewhat down, grinning and waving. He only stops to greet a mother and her toddler (*nice celebrity move, bro*), just enough so that any pictures and video that makes it onto social media will at least portray *the* J.D. Church as somewhat humble, and maybe a little bit shy.

One bodyguard sticks to his side while the other retrieves his luggage at baggage claim. There's already a vehicle waiting when they've gotten the luggage. Pretty nice, not a limousine, but rather one of the many new Tesla models being recommended to ride app drivers. Just like that, in under 25 minutes, Church is in the safety of a vehicle like a pro. He navigates the confusion and stress of JFK with ease, and once he's in that backseat, I bet he's breathing better, probably chatting with the bodyguards, nothing too intimate. Likely today's schedule of events. It's going to be a long week in the city. Church hasn't visited since last year, which means everyone earning anything off his brand name is going to ensure that they get the most out of him while he's here.

The Tesla is easily lost in traffic. One wrong turn, and he's no longer in my sights. Not that I'm too worried. When you have access like I do, every email and text message shared between agent and author, author and editor, author and publicist, it doesn't really matter if his driver makes a right at the intersection and I am stuck at a red light.

I know where he's staying.

I know what route the driver will likely take.

And best of all, I know which room the publisher has booked. You see, an author like Church doesn't want to go for the penthouse suite. No, imagine if word got out that he enjoys such lavishness. He wants to remain grounded in reality. Just any ol' room will do. So that means seventh floor, third door on the left.

Well, good, because I just so happen to have reserved the room next door. Modest price for Manhattan, too. So, I take my own route, side streets and then over the bridge. I'll get there around the same time he does, but even so, I won't be spotted.

I won't even be in the same line.

Where they get dropped off, I drive by, choosing to park the car myself in the hotel's own subterranean parking garage. When I finally make it out of the elevator and step foot into the lobby, he'll be almost finished checking in. Not that Church has any of those details. His two bodyguards handle the business while Church focuses on his phone, presumably he's texting with, I don't know, maybe Pendel, or his young assistant. Yeah, probably the latter actually. She seems like the loyal type, never dropping the ball. You'd have to be if you last more than six months as Pendel's assistant.

The bodyguards aren't paid to stick around.

I'll wait at the bar, sipping from a seltzer, while they chat and then part ways. I'll leave the glass almost full, walking the length of the lobby casually enough not to catch any looks. At the elevator block, I'll stand near him, but not near enough. The elevators always offer their own preemptive cues. People rush off the elevator and there's always a few that clamor to get on first, when really the worst spots are in the back of the elevator.

Church knows this. He is much calmer and nondescript than any fan might think. Though recognizable when one's read even a single paragraph of his work, he could easily pass off as just another middle-aged white man. Yet even at this hotel, he battles the hellos, the various fans asking for an autograph. Still, I wait. I'm patient like that.

Does it seem like I've done this before?

Is it so obvious?

In the elevator, we stand next to each other, both staring up at the numbers rolling past. In the hushed silence of an elevator, you'd think I'd be nervous; Church *is* standing right next to me.

Yet no, it'll be okay. I've played this out in my head. Everything goes according to plan.

When we both get off on the same floor, I know well to make a show of how ironic that we're "neighbors."

He grins and nods, "Seems like it." I see it in his eyes, the exhaustion.

We're both fumbling for our key cards when I make that connection, a simple and so very common ask, yet the one he will soon regret.

"Umm," I start and then stop, coming off shy. "Could I...?"

He nods, exhaling deeply, a quick draw from his pocket revealing an expensive pen, "Autograph? Sure."

"Thanks so much," I say, reaching into my pocket. My turn to grin, and it's genuine because I know he's expecting a book.

CHAPTER 5

That feeling in the pit of his stomach, it could be whatever —fear, stress, anxiety. Really, Pendel's more inclined to believe it's the beginning of a heart attack or stroke. This long since inking a deal, and with his highest-earning client? It's a miracle he hasn't broken out into hives yet. Seriously, what the fuck is going on?

He isn't in a position to have a dry spell.

Never mind the warning signs of an impending merger and a handful of publishing imprints being restructured, absorbed, and very plainly cannibalized to repair a company bottom line; in his 12 years as an agent, he's garnered deals on a weekly basis, often so many he can't keep track of what's been announced and what has yet to get its little marketplace deal announcement.

When Marina tells him that Church is unreachable, he knows it's a lie. His author is not only *very* reachable but also likely in the city right now, the same damn city, and yet he can't even get a text or a call.

Pendel picks up the phone, a cold call. This is serious. Hendrix hasn't been responsive, and that is enough to be viewed as a sign of disrespect.

"Anything else?" Marina remains poised, on guard at the office door.

"No," he says, batting her away with his hand. Then he remembers something and calls out to her while she is still within earshot, "But the queries!"

Way ahead of him. She gives him a deadline, "I'll have the latest to you by the end of the week." Same as always.

"Good," he mumbles, newly alone in his office. "Good..."

Hendrix must be on the line, the phone continuing to dial, the tone repeating like further proof of him being cold-shouldered by what he had thought was his biggest lead. Pendel curses to himself and hangs up. Immediately, he dials again, this time he goes right to the publisher, who picks up on the third ring.

"Henry Pendel, how the hell are you this afternoon?!" This Jonathan Sharpe, he's always traded with such positivity it borders on plastic and overtly fake. "Love the fall weather finally coming in."

Pendel can't stand it, "Never mind all that. Where are we on the latest Church manuscript? We have quite the ticking clock on this, and I haven't heard back from your editor, Hendrix."

Where Sharpe may deal in false positivity, Pendel's frequent threatening, bordering on aggressive advances are the stuff of legend. Sharpe laughs, "I can say that we're all loving the book. It may be J.D. Church's best yet!"

"You're not answering me," says Pendel. "I'm holding out on this for the sake of our history. We're talking preempt, for an author like J.D. Church. That just doesn't happen, hmm? I can go to S&S or even Cachet and they'll pull all the stops, give the biggest offer possible. But here we are. How many books have we brokered together... eight? And now, of all times, you all are ghosting me?"

After a brief pause, Sharpe's suddenly more evenly toned, the positivity snuffed, "We are not ghosting you, Henry. We never have. We are in fact working with both the editorial and marketing departments to best assess the quality of the offer. We aren't taking any of this lightly, I guarantee you."

"Stop talking PR talk," Pendel sighs. "This is me. Tell it straight. I know his sales numbers. This can't have anything to do with a P&L statement not adding up."

Sharpe clears his throat, a tell, "Actually, it's not that at all."

"Out with it," Pendel says, tapping his finger against the receiver. "There must be a reason you haven't just pounced."

"Right," Sharpe replies. "Short version is there have been some allegations that have come to light on behalf of Church. It looks like it happened many years ago, back when he was a professor and not yet the 'J.D. Church' we all know like the back of our hand."

"Okay..." That feeling again.

Hives.

Pendel's entire body visibly shakes.

Dry mouth, eye twitch.

Numbness in left arm.

A stroke, maybe an aneurysm.

Sharpe's voice fades out and then back in with a slight ringing in Pendel's ear, "... and our lawyers have begun investigating the severity of the allegations. Though there could be a statute of limitations to defamation, if there is evidence that he was sexually abusive and predatory to some of his female students, there could be legal action taken."

Pendel is livid, "Oh please. They come out of the woodwork when one's standing tall at the top of the mountain. How many copies did *December Falls* sell last year?"

"Well, the allegations are quite—"

"How many?" Pendel won't let Sharpe worm out of it.

"BookScan, last I checked was..."

"It could sell a million copies," Pendel says. "Not even a year in the market, and it's out in dozens of languages, a film adaptation with David Fincher at the helm, this is his biggest novel yet, and guess what?" He holds on to that question.

"What?"

"*December Falls* was a preempt. I gave it to you guys. Hendrix got first dibs."

"I understand, Henry. I really do. We're in an odd situation and..."

Ringing in his ear.

He groans, blood boiling.

Pendel snaps, "Look! Nobody reads anymore. I'm almost positive nobody picks up a book simply to read for pleasure. People buy books because they want to be part of something that the author has already propelled into the media stratosphere. The book they buy is sacred, like a new spell capable of making their lives more exciting for a couple days. And it can't be just any author. It takes a special voice, a writer that can be more than the 98%. Most books last year sold less than 3,000 copies. Don't you get it? We aren't moving books. We're moving prospects. The writing itself is the least profitable part. Moving prospects means we're talking scandals, media spinning the story, and deals—speaking gigs, classes, seminars, films, television shows... there's no limit to an empire once it is branded effectively."

Or, to put it simply, Pendel can see the allegations as publicity. Publicity always pays.

"Look, I'm leveling with you," Sharpe says. "Hendrix is Church's champion. There will be a book deal, and soon. I promise you. It's more like we're waiting for what our legal department decides, and how to work through this mess. I hear you loud and clear. Things do need to change. We, and by we, I mean me, I believe truly in people getting second chances."

"Church is of an older generation," Pendel says, coming up with excuses. "What they saw as predatory behavior, maybe he saw as being flirtatious. He didn't know."

Pendel didn't know.

Silence on the other line. Pendel exhales deeply. He could use a drink. "If anything, you should be adding a few extra zeroes to that number," Pendel says.

"I hear you," says Sharpe. "Expect an email by EOD."

CHAPTER 6

I love the look on his face. Proof that someone so conditioned to being recognized in public, used to signing autographs everywhere he goes, is still capable of surprise.

Perhaps *pleasantly* surprised?

"So sorry," I say. Utilizing a mixture of shy and clumsy, especially when you take the time and care to condition a look (meaning dress—opt for a nice shirt, nice haircut, a nice smile) that thwarts any suspicion, I attach the apology with good-natured hyperbole: "Go figure. I've been a fan for over a decade and have all of your books on my shelves, even that rare hard-to-find novella *Night Moves,* which only had, I think, a thousand copies printed, and I even went to that AWP across the country the year where you were on a panel with other writers about conditioning oneself in the face of public opinion, and I stood in line for like an hour before I had to leave the line because I had to go help staff a table at the bookfair, and then I even went to your book launch for *December Falls* in the city but was too nervous to face you, so, I just listened to the reading and conversation, just another person in the audience, and then I left with my copy unsigned like a coward and regretted it for days, and now here you are, standing right in front of me..." I point at his hotel room door, "We're neighbors in a liminal space! And I don't have anything but this," I have my moleskin, a diary, held outward like an offering, "with me for your autograph."

Exhale. Note that it did the trick. He's overwhelmed but charmed. I've proven that I'm a rabid fan, and like any author, they can't risk losing someone so supportive. Unlike rockstars and actors, authors connect purely through the intimacy of reading. Once that level of trust is shattered, it's hard to regain. It's not like some actor ending up in rehab after a meltdown and then playing the role of a wounded character a few projects later, or a rockstar turning out to be a sleazebag, yet remains at the height of their powers, mostly because they were always a superficial persona to begin with. Authors tell stories, and stories have the potential to teach readers how to survive the ongoing story of their lives.

"Calm down," he says. "It's cool." He takes my moleskin. "Life is weird that way."

"It is," I say, intentionally out of breath.

He's flipping through the first couple of pages, "Is this... your diary?"

I frown, a little bit bashful, "Is that weird?"

We exchange eye contact and then he clicks his pen, "Yeah, it's weird. But I dig it."

There we are, first contact, in a hallway in some Manhattan hotel. J.D. Church stops on a page, bad poetry, and I see that gesture of judgment. Everyone's got to start somewhere. Words don't just pour out of a mind readymade; you got to bleed a little bit so that they may scream off the page.

"What's your name?"

"Oh!" Now it's about giving a whole lot of nerves, maybe a little stutter as I tell him, "My-my name is Alex."

"Alex," he says, vision trained to a page at random. Then he says one of a half dozen things he tells everyone as he scribbles his signature and accompanying "stay scared" message: "So which one did you in first?"

He's asking about the book title of note.

Always doing his marketing research, a little dragging, seeing what can be unearthed from the depths of narcissism. I already have his full life story memorized, right down to a lesser known fact that he faked most of his publicized childhood, and though the names are real—mom's name is Margot, father's name is Charles—everything else, including the now well-regarded and infinitely quoted stuff like his first childhood fear ("I was afraid of strangers long before I became afraid of the unknown"), is a fiction all its own. I know all about his secret safety net, an inheritance from his aunt who passed away from cancer, the only relative he was ever close to, and how, though he did work a few retail jobs, a year at an Amazon fulfillment center, and then finally as a professor at two separate state colleges, he never needed the funds. The money went first into fueling his budding alcoholism and then, after he got sober, again, made into a public story that ended with it being relatable and edifying for his entire fanbase: *I'm flawed. A person is flawed; they are like the best characters in a book, flawed and complex, a contradiction waiting to be found and figured out.*

His significant savings went into a marketing fund for his first half-dozen books. And I even know all about what's taken the whisper networks a decade to dig up, the allegations, grooming and being a sexual predator to young female college students, many of them aspiring writers looking up to Church. I know the number currently is five but will climb to 18 in a month. I know he's worried, which could be the real reason for having two bodyguards, being so hush-hush; the past comes back, like any good story, the details that direct a character and plot circle back to complete its thread. What I know, yet he doesn't, is that he won't need to worry about his career. He won't be seeing the full wrath of his misdeeds. When I'm replying with personal details rather than a book title, it sets an entirely different sort of tone.

"I think it was when you said you worked at an Amazon fulfillment center and stole from 'the man' as a means of making ends meet," I say.

He almost doesn't hear me, or rather, he doesn't want to believe that I brought up something so personal, something hidden behind layers of time and fabrication.

"What was that now?"

I laugh, "I'm just nervous; that's all!"

Suddenly he's nervous too, and I deflate the situation by turning our attention back to the moleskin. Sure enough, the same prepackaged annotation, "Stay scared."

"There's a lot to be scared about," I say.

He grins, but when he agrees, "Yeah, the world is weird and full of monsters," I can see his mind working through the sequence of events.

The moleskin back in my hand, I turn to my door, keycard pressed to the sensor. The doorknob beeps. Turning it, I step partly inside the darkened room, "Thank you for the autograph! You've made my day. No, my year!"

Church remains in the hallway, "Yeah. Yeah of course."

My door closes as I see him fumble for his keycard.

"Stay scared," I whisper.

Chapter 7

What was it about being patient? The moment he ends the call, Pendel's flagging Marina down, sending a quick email, not even a full sentence *office in five*, he's already losing track of some valuable advice. When she's there in three, he's already mid-task, telling her that he "needs to raise the dead."

Marina doesn't follow. "Excuse me?"

A glazed over look on his face. He chuckles, "Never mind. You never did connect with my morbid sense of humor. Good thing you're cute."

"Guess not," she says. She scrolls through her tablet, anticipating the next command.

"What was that editor's name again?" he asks, absentmindedly clicking around in his contacts list. "We're finalizing a deal today, even if it means diving into the dredges."

"You mean Emily?"

"Emily?" He doesn't find an Emily in his contacts list, at least not one that is in an editorial role. Pendel gets an email notification, one that he ignores. Just because he deleted the email from Moyer doesn't mean the message hasn't been made.

"I can't believe you still can't remember her name," she says. "It's Emily Mills. She's the new big shot at FSG. You should remember the name; she's gathering a real great catalog of authors."

In one ear and out the other, Pendel nods, "Emily Mills. Thanks. I have her number, right?"

This time Marina doesn't bother. It's just a waste of her time. This is trademark Pendel treading the byline and latest trends. He's under a lot of stress. He's got a reputation and a hefty list of clients to take care of, especially when it comes to selling. These are the most common excuses Marina tends to find a degree of understanding. And when that doesn't work, she defaults to it being her day gig. It doesn't pay well ($39k after taxes, fun stuff), but all her friends lately, especially those in the industry, have been losing their jobs. Between the impending merger(s) and artificial intelligence, staffers have lost all sense of job security.

The phone number is given, though Marina makes a lone comment, "Emily's quicker via email," and she's back at her desk. Pendel likes to call people. It has everything to do with catching them off guard.

Emily picks up after the sixth ring, "Emily Mills, hello."

"Hello there... Emily," he says, not bothering to give his name.

"Hello!"

No reply. He expects her to recognize his voice. What follows is a silence bordering on awkwardness.

"This is Emily," she says again, because what else does one do besides consider hanging up the phone?

When nothing changes, she adds the requisite inquiry, "May I help you?"

"I'd hope so," Pendel says. "You do know who this is, right? We have some pressing matters to discuss."

"Oh, of course, yes. This is... Mr. Pendel, correct?"

"Yes," he says, disappointed.

"Hi there!" The false sense of excitement is paper thin, altogether too obvious to just shrug off. "I enjoyed our meeting today!"

"It's okay," he says. "You can dial it down a few. Last thing I need is a headache."

"Oh, well all right."

He's already forgotten about the boilerplate, "I'm calling because it seems to me that you're forgetting something."

"I am...?"

There's another email. Quick glance and he sees the name Alexander Moyer, and again, he notes the name, yet continues to ignore every attempt. It's up to the lawyer now. He treats it like any other stalker or invasive hanger-on: Give them nothing, and then, should they continue, give them the full extent of legal wrath. This call, like most things that he does that qualify as petty, is designed to make Pendel feel better, when really, every email spikes his anxiety, producing an influx of stress and worry.

Everything seems to be falling apart. What the hell is going on?

"You haven't sent in your offer," he says.

Target locked, he needs nothing more right now than to make a young editor sweat it out, squirm in their seat.

"Oh, well, I was under the impress... umm, the impression that..." Mills trips over her words. "I'd have some time to..." Her brief pause has everything to do with carefully selecting the right choice of words in this delicate, tense situation. "Time to... well..." A single beat, and then she says, "I would need a few days to read."

"You've had long enough," he says. "I've already told you this is going to be huge. I can see the book on all the lists, in everyone's minds, its cover becoming iconic, a gem of a cultural moment. I've given you a golden ticket, so now you got to pay up."

"Mr. Pendel, I cannot rightly make an offer on a book I have not read," she says, before immediately back-tracking due to intimidation. "What I'm trying to say is... I need to read the book so I can come up with an accurate enough figure to offer."

"Let me help you out," he says. "It'll save you time. Maybe even gets you climbing up that corporate ladder a bit quicker. What you do with this debut is you offer me $50k, lowball, so that your bosses and the marketing department don't immediately say no. $50k split into installments is nothing. You'll look like you know what you're doing."

Emily Mills knows what she's doing. Still, he continues, refusing to give her a single moment to speak. "I'll take that $50k and double it. $100k. Still pretty modest, especially when Kawada becomes the next biggest thing, which he will, and the first printing sells out, *which it will*, and by then, $100k will look like $100 when looking back at the investment. On the other side of the deal, we'll both come out on top, you'll get a promotion, and suddenly everyone will believe in you unequivocally. Maybe then you'll get the books you really want."

Pendel isn't a bad person. He doesn't mean to be so cutthroat and downright mean, but he must put his emotions somewhere, and he's never been great at sitting and processing his feelings. And really, this isn't the first time he's groomed an editor. Hendrix de Leon had to start somewhere. One morning he received a call from one Henry Richmond Pendel, and by the end of it, Hendrix had made an offer on a book he had never read; Pendel inked yet another deal (the good ol' days when he often ended a month so above his expectations that he gleefully took that extra-long weekend upstate, took twice as many vacations than normal, often right in the middle of the busiest time of the year for trade publishing, just because), and Hendrix became a made editor. Not that Pendel gatekeeps or even has full control over anything. Really, he's just good at what he does. Ask him and he'll tell you, *Yeah, I'm probably a sociopath.* Laughter would follow, but along with the joke, a nugget of truth would carry forward.

Emily is speechless.

"Email me the offer within the hour," he says. "Then the boilerplate. Let's get this complete by day's end, hmm?"

She manages a reply, "Will do..."

"Good," he says. "Don't fuck up this opportunity."

He hangs up. In every sense of the term, he leaves her hanging. Leave it up to Emily to figure out how to make this all happen before the end of the business day. He'll enjoy thinking about how stressful the remainder of her day will be. It gets him through all the unknowns, all the uncertainty, and it helps him delete yet another email from Moyer without thinking about it. It's nothing. Reminder: This has everything to do with him feeling in control and nothing at all about the poor young editor giving it her all.

That's what he tells himself.

Repeat it enough times and eventually you'll start to believe.

Chapter 8

Before I bother knocking, I dart off an email, one that implicates his agent. No big deal, just a little note that says he has the power to stop this. All he needs to do is email me back, hear me out, see through the clearing, and understand that he's made and continues to make a big mistake. He's losing out on so much money, and soon, he'll be losing out on one of his biggest clients.

Maybe all his clients...

But let's not get ahead of ourselves. A story can always benefit from a few notes.

We're going to workshop the key details.

A little tap-tap on the door, Church sees me standing there, and he could easily not open the door, which could be the solution, real armor for an incoming personal attack, but he's going to pry. Undoubtedly, he must wonder, a fellow devotee of the weird, how crazy can this fan interaction get?

He uses the door as a shield, barely ajar. "Did you find a book for me to sign?"

"Yeah," I flash a smile. "I actually have your latest right here!"

When he sees the bound manuscript, things change quickly.

"How did you get that?"

"This?" The title page reads: *The Renegades*. "I just finished reading it on the flight over!"

"No," he shakes his head. "I don't care. Wait..." Composure failing in five, four, three, two... "Nobody should have that except my agent."

My agent.

I've always found it so... possessive. Like being owner and owned, the author is more likely to say "my agent" than an agent to say "my author." Well, some agents do it more flippantly, but usually it's only tossed around by an agent if they are particularly proud of the author. *My author.*

"Oh right," I laugh. "That's right. So sorry. This must all be so confusing. You see... your agent sent me the manuscript!"

It washes over him right as I jam my boot between the door and frame.

In a low whisper, I offer my first piece of feedback, "You know, it runs a little long. You could stand to get right to the action, less info dumping, more death."

And then we're inside the room, door locked, no one any wiser, and he's coming apart like anyone would under the circumstances, tripping over his own clumsy feet, on the floor and crawling away from... me? Come on now, be a little more original. But give him the benefit of the doubt. That's what the workshop is for.

I toss the bound manuscript onto the bed. "At a hefty 810 pages, and who knows how many will be in the final hardcover, you manage to keep the group of survivors away from danger for 65% of it. There are only three action scenes? Only one survivor dies? Church, you really need to double down on the war. It's supposed to be a climate-centric civil war, hmm?"

I rush over and grab him before he can send for help and put him in a headlock. "You see, something as simple as a headlock. Why didn't any of the soldiers or survivors get in each other's faces? What happened to all the grit and grime from your other books? Instead, you have them go on and on, talking up a snoozefest."

Apply enough pressure, keep the hold locked, and he'll begin to nod off. His body goes limp. "Exactly my point. Your book put me to sleep."

While he's out, I restrain him to the desk chair with zip ties. A ball gag around the mouth works well enough. Time is certainly valuable. He's out for around ten minutes. Enough time for me to gather my notes.

I'd love to impress him.

Give him something to reconsider this late in the process.

Nearly out on submission, and J.D. Church decides to pull the novel, do some more editing, all because of my feedback. Imagine!

It's a good fantasy.

But he's awake and I'm not finding a whole lot to critique, at least nothing that really warrants the effort.

"You see, I think when it comes down to it... I just find your novel to be, well, unimaginative." That's the cold hard truth. "You've always been so clever and so poignant, so on-the-pulse with cultural issues, but this climate horror post-apocalyptic whatever-the-fuck, it's just... boring. I really don't have much else to comment on."

It's like in the movies. He makes noises and struggles to break free. And, like in the movies, his own struggle results in some self-sabotage. So swiftly he shifts to playing the victim. I haven't even done anything, yet.

The chair crashes to the hotel room floor. On his side like that, I have direct access to his arms. I can see the daisy chain of purple-blue veins, his pale flesh untouched and unedited.

I brought along with me a few items. I'd like to think of them as part of the process; everyone's got a favorite. Pen to paper, there's always something in hand.

"Found this gem at a specialty shop," I say. "It's what I work with best."

He can't see the large blade in my hand. He can't see the lye, vials of bleach, and other liquids I carry with me, just in case. Probably for the better. I need him lucid.

Back to the manuscript, I know exactly which pages to cut. Using the tip of the blade, I cut a handful of pages from the beginning, a handful more from the middle, and then a whole lot from the end. A post-apocalyptic novel where the last half is just the two survivors talking and reminiscing? Complete with footnotes?

Cut.

He screams, and I have to give him a warning, "Yo, keep it down or else we'll have to cut this workshop short."

I find a few areas, forearms and the soft underside of his armpits.

"These could all stand to use a rewrite," I say, taking each page and folding it three ways before offering the final insulating fold of his skin. The pages fit perfectly in each wound, thank you very much. I measured the length, thinking about trim sizes and other production details. Unlike Church, I've outlined and planned this all out. Still, we got a few more cuts, in some cases, whole chapters. After a few more, he stops making a sound.

Church passes out from the pain. It's a shame, really. He could use the feedback. But that's okay. I'll keep cutting until I find something worth keeping. After the arms, then the legs. Save the best for last, the chest, namely the heart. The liquids will come in handy.

Guess it's up to me to fix this story.

J.D. Church is kind of a letdown. I had hoped for my debut to be far more poetic, more than what's on the page. It's the reason I started with the best, a brand name, the author and king of an entire genre. Instead, it's down to blood loss and torture.

How boring.

I guess there's always the next one.

His body of work is impressive, really it is, but when it comes to the body, it's like everything else: You cut and peel away to the skeleton underneath, and it all looks the same.

Chapter 9

It's nearly 6 PM and the only one of his calls that has been returned is from Pendel's lawyer. His assistant should really go home for the day, but Pendel keeps Marina around because he expects that offer from the young editor whose name he still can't quite remember.

"Anything yet?"

She peeks into his office, "Not yet." It is followed by the reminder, "But Benji is on line two. He's still on line two."

Pendel doesn't say anything. His inbox refreshes, revealing yet another email. Moyer.

"He's been waiting," she says. "You do know he's paid by the hour... right?"

"Get me what's-her-name on the phone," he says, changing the subject. "The nerve, letting such a perfect opportunity slip away."

"Sure thing." Marina shuts the door and less than five minutes later, line three lights up. Like a good assistant, she never forgets a request or task. Leave line one open. Just in case. He's left multiple messages. It's troubling when a client goes silent, especially one who keeps his cash flow steady and comfortable.

Getting into character, he holds his breath and then—"So where's my offer? Was it misplaced somewhere?"

"Pendel, we have much to discuss."

Wrong line. The lawyer.

Shit. The last thing Pendel wants is to talk "terms" and possible recourse. It's a pulverizing reminder of the danger surrounding him from all sides. If only he knew the full extent of what was unfolding. There's no going back now. He's got to talk about it sometime.

"Yes, we do," he says, feeling the stress manifesting as an ache in his jaw. "Lay it on me. Understand that I hired you because you don't waterboard me with legalese. Let's keep it that way."

"Understood," Benji says. "I have gone through the communications you've sent me. They've all been emails, correct?"

"Correct," he says. "But I do suspect that this stalker, this writer, this whoever, has been inside my house."

"How certain are you?"

"Things moved. Things missing. Personal space ruined and disrespected," he says. "That's got to count for something."

"It gets a little tricky." The lawyer dives into the short version, "You can file a restraining order, which, obviously, is a done deal. However, outside of that, unless there's more, I won't have much for you."

He gets a text message. Before he checks, Pendel must know, "What's the guy's deal? This Moyer? What does he want?"

"Same as any writer," Benji says. "He wants your attention, your validation, and ultimately he wants you to sign him and represent his work."

Representation. Like submission, it is a term veiled and layered in the interpersonal dramatics of author and agent. To be represented becomes more than the brokering of a deal; it becomes an author receiving an agent's "stamp of approval." To write something, an author must learn to live with something; to submit, the author must learn to give something away. For Pendel there might not be much of a difference.

"Stalking and making threats," he chuckles. "That'll really inspire me to give his query another look."

"The remainder of the correspondence, hmm..." He can hear Benji typing away at his keyboard. "Yeah, I wouldn't worry too much about it. If you haven't looked, I would keep it that way."

"No interest," says Pendel. "I'd be more inclined to delete them."

"Don't do that." A lawyer thrives on documentation and paperwork. "Forward them first, at least."

"No need to tell me twice." He sent them to Benji. Well, whenever he remembers, that is. Some went right into trash and he's not going to look back.

He gets a text message. One look at the sender's name and his heart skips a beat.

"Okay Benji, update me if and when you can do more about this... this matter."

"Sure thing I'll email with—"

Pendel ends the call.

"About fucking time," he mutters to himself. He taps the screen of his phone and darts off a reply, "Don't scare me like that."

Church is finally coming up for air. Pendel is instantly relieved.

And then Marina reenters the office, "Emily has sent an offer!"

Pendel claps his hands together, saying it again, even more enthusiastically than before, "About fucking time!"

Notification. A new text message from Church.

"So what are we looking at?" Pendel says, gaze fixed on his phone.

Church offers an apology—everyone always apologizes to Pendel—and then says, "Can't seem to get a moment's peace. Being recognized. Can't get used to it."

Pendel always knows what to say, "You're famous. A public figure. There's a parasocial element, and best of all, you have written more masterpieces than a hundred writers combined."

Flattery. It always works on an author.

"She offered $50k," says Marina.

He loves this part, feeling like some conductor guiding a deal through its penultimate crescendo. "Draft an email countering with 100k."

"Double? Wow," Marina grins. "That's... bold."

Pendel looks up from his phone, "Counter with $100k. Make it quick. I may need to head out soon."

She rushes out of the office, “On it!”

Church texts back, “A masterpiece is subjective. I hear you.”

“The sales numbers tell all,” he says. “Now what’s the status on the latest MASTERPIECE?”

No word from Hendrix. No word from Sharpe.

Pendel doesn’t back down, though.

“Incorporating some last-minute feedback,” Church says. “Should be done tonight.”

Good news. Pendel offers to meet up for brunch tomorrow, their favorite place, meaning Church’s go-to when he’s in the city. Pendel doesn’t care where they go if it ensures that he has the latest manuscript in hand when he finally gets Hendrix on the line.

“Can do,” Church says.

“Great,” he says.

Marina returns to the office with yet another offer. Pendel won’t take anything less than $100k. He turns it into a bit of a tutorial. They counter with $80k and explain how staying strong at $100k will quickly run out their bargaining power. Soon they’ll be pressed up against $100k and the finer details, like number of installments, sub rights, and other gritty details that publisher and agent fight over because, you see...

“The gritty details grow to become the greenest pastures,” he winks.

Pendel’s attention moves to the Kawada deal. This young new editor, he may finally remember her name. Emily Mills counters their counter with $95k, which they refuse and expectantly stand at $100k.

At 6:45 PM, Mills gives them a call. Pendel picks up and it’s more of the same, only this time Marina is in earshot. He makes a show of it, same sternness, and borderline use of fear tactics to influence the young editor into the deal they want. The tutorial concludes with an accepted offer, Mills sending the contract, no longer mere boilerplate terms, now fully customized to the accepted terms.

“And that,” Pendel reclines in his chair, hands behind his head, “is how you launch an author’s career.”

Marina is impressed, but any additional admiration is cut short when Pendel reminds her that she will be the one to facilitate the contract.

"I'm off to enjoy the night," he says, gathering his phone and other belongings.

Both Marina and Mills have another hour, bouncing emails back and forth, signing on the dotted line, getting it all prepped for the deal announcement post-haste. Everybody knows Pendel doesn't like to wait.

On the way out of the office, Church sends another text message, "Looking forward to it!"

Years of texting off and on, Church never being much for any other mood than morose, straight and to the point. Business first. Did that really sound like his author?

Pendel doesn't think anything of it.

Chapter 10

I only keep the good parts. The title is functional. *The Renegades.* Same with the characters: A trio of survivors in an eco-disaster, pulverizing civil war to end all wars, is enough to work with. Yet I still can't believe how such a great writer turned a solid foundation into a snoozefest.

My neighbor has a lot to think about after our workshop. I left him soaking in the tub. I find that a nice, good burn really opens the senses, gets the imagination racing. It's only a matter of time before the words find themselves on the page, fully rendered.

Me, I'm so inspired right now.

My time with such a great author is more than enough to inspire me.

I paid for the hotel room, so I might as well make a little bit of a residency out of it, right?

"I'm positively sorry for not being responsive."

Pendel, do you know who you're talking to?

"Incorporating some last-minute feedback. Should be done tonight."

Well, not quite actually. He'll need a bit more time, but housekeeping's got it covered. They'll find his body before we meet for brunch. I've put a do-not-disturb over the doorknob. The smell will get to them, maybe some complaints from the floor below about a leak. The porcelain of a bathtub is quite resilient, but the liquid solution I use in my process is more intense than most. Part of my so-called calling card, my modus operandi.

I leave something behind.

Every author holds a desire for that brand of legacy.

Flipping through what's left of the manuscript, I think I'll save the chapters that Church left behind. The title, the premise, like I said, it's all serviceable, but I'll do one better: I'm going to take the chapters, the scenes, the character moments that come to life, the moments that make a story more than the sum of its parts.

Pendel's happy about it.

I make sure to tell him, "I'm inspired. I'm doing my best work yet!"

He makes plans. Brunch. Sure thing. Not like I didn't already anticipate his moves. It's part of the process; we'll be texting throughout the night. He leaves the office around 7 PM, drops by a nearby dive bar to grab a few without being spotted. Then he's back to the Village, the same apartment. Wish I could be there to hang around, be in his company, but not tonight. I got so much work to do! There's so much to look over in this manuscript. To think: How to make this work best? And then there's tomorrow and the weekend. After the weekend, we've got the week to follow. Pendel's in good hands. He may think I'm a stalker, but come on, don't we all deserve a better story than that?

"I have another idea," I say, via text.

"Tell me!"

Pendel lacks any bonds. He doesn't have any friends. His friends are the surface level connections and transactional conversations with his clients. The poor guy. Still has all those photos hanging on his walls of his ex. What was his name... Whenever I forget, I check Pendel's Instagram. Charles. Charlie. Often referred to as Chuck. He was a writer too. His last known whereabouts remain unknown. That is, if you keep to Pendel's feed.

Chuck is now Clara, living well on the West Coast. Has a great partner by the looks of it. Still writing, but there doesn't seem to be any interest in publishing the work—trauma from nearly a decade near the gossip, the wheeling and dealing, the industry at max.

So many stories. Which ones to tell...

"I had the idea on the plane ride," I say, a story forming out of thin air. "It's why I didn't reply. I was too busy jotting everything down. So anyway, I had this idea, a sort of retelling of an earlier book of mine, *An Outsider*, but modernized, with the protagonist in a Robinson Crusoe situation when they lose their cell phone and suddenly become completely invisible to everyone."

Of course, he loves the idea.

I'm not about to tell him that it's a J.G. Ballard novel. Well, except for the phone. *Concrete Island* almost completely.

"*The Renegades* might irk some people," I say.

He won't let a client think less of themselves or their work. Pendel sends back a long paragraph that is so reassuring, I almost tear up. He is such a good champion. So what if he hasn't read the book? He puts his reputation on the line, blind to every word.

And so let it be.

It's beautiful, really.

He doesn't know my full potential. It's up to me, the author, to tell the story, make it undeniable.

He asks me if the manuscript is done.

Representation. My author, my agent. Together, hands held into submission.

"In due time."

Pendel explains how he hopes to garner a multiple book deal, seven figures, giving "me" the room to write this new book, the new idea, and therefore to continue "doing what you do best." To that, I take another step, just a little tease. See if he notices.

"Already living my best life," I say.

J.D. Church is living his best life. One broken equals another's breakthrough.

Pendel is at his desk, alone in that apartment. I like to hold on to that image, not because it's saddening. No, not at all. It's because he's texting with one person, undivided attention. One person, nobody else. And that person is me.

I'll continue to keep him company.

Ambition. Pendel begins to lower his guard as evening turns to night. The alcohol loosens his tongue and he gets to talking about his career, his legacy, the dollar amount he hopes to die with, a number so high, I can only text back emojis. Pendel's own legacy is about leaving behind an impression. When it's "Church's" turn to talk legacy, it's all about the work-in-progress.

"I would like to finish all the books I plan to write before it's all said and done."

How many is that? The lonely and weakened agent wants to know.

"It's always changing," I say, a truth, one harsh enough that might catch a writer vulnerable enough like shrapnel. Pendel texts back an "LOL." Is he actually laughing on the other end? How many sips before the end of that drink and the beginning of the next pour?

An offering of assurance, I tell him, "I'll leave behind enough projects to ensure a healthy posthumous career."

"That's why you're my favorite client!"

In death, ownership remains.

My author.

My agent.

My idea.

My body of work.

My work-in-progress.

"An author leaves behind a world for their readers. An agent leaves behind unfinished work." He shouldn't be telling a client such things, but I appreciate this trial period, a little taste of how our relationship will work on a professional and personal level.

"I have another idea," I say.

"I love it. I love the hustle."

Tongue so loose he's one half-step away from love. And then it hits me, and I have all that I need to see this through. Pendel doesn't know it yet, but he's on the verge of a career-high, a new accomplishment. He's about to sign the client of a lifetime.

Brunch tomorrow. He'll be so happy to see me.

The only work-in-progress that ever remains unfinished is yourself.

CHAPTER 11

Columbia alum **Brendon Kawada**'s debut **MECHANICAL ANIMALS**, a novel about an epic struggle across time between two star-crossed lovers that may in fact also be vampires, leaving behind a trail of broken hearts and drained bodies, to **Emily Mills** at **FSG**, in a six-figure deal, in an exclusive submission, by **Henry Richmond Pendel** at **Cooper Willis Endeavor** (world English).

How wonderful it is to be the current topic of conversation, in the minds of the tastemakers and industry talkers. Pendel lives for these moments. Surely the money and the liquidity of being a top 5 agent in collective deals industrywide helps with cash flow and financial freedom, but the real rush comes from the praise and occasional jealousy that comes from his peers. He loves seeing everyone clamor over a 60-word deal announcement; mere mention of the premise and the deal figure is enough to have dozens of editors in other territories and industries crawling over to him, asking about sub rights, film options, the whole gamut.

Certainly helps when battling a hangover. Pendel calls a car and gets to the office by 9:30 AM. He's running on fumes and waiting for the painkillers to kick in when he gets the first email, this one from an editor he's done work with previously, one that sold Pendel short, believing he wouldn't find deals for a few riskier and controversial clients. He still has the receipts, email exchanges where the editor said, *It's just too dark, and I like dark*, and, *You'll be lucky if you find a home for it in the indie and small press world*, and, *If it isn't with the Big Five then it doesn't really exist.* The editor's name, he doesn't bother. It's a name among other names, all of them judging based on perception. Right about now, Pendel is among the select few agents that has been able to secure six-figure deals in the last four months due to the industrywide dry spell. He has broken free of the worry, and now, you better believe he's going to relish every pandering and congratulatory email.

Wow, this sounds amazing. The editor says after Pendel replies to the broader initial congrats. *What else do you have in the docket? I'm actively acquiring for next fall. I'll put yours as top priority.*

Pendel's got him right where he wants him. First, he waits nearly a half hour before replying, which establishes the impression that Pendel is busy, has more pressing matters than this editor, and then when he does reply, he settles for a calm and disengaged, *Great! I'll consult my list and see where your sensibility might fit in.*

Done. Nothing more, nothing less. He might as well have said, *Go fuck yourself.*

Pendel doesn't intentionally hold grudges; it's more like the consistent nonstop 12-hour days, the chase and hustle for lateral movement in this industry, have warped his priorities. Really, it's just too much fun to see those who had once sold you short, treated you unfairly, coming back acting like nothing's happened. A fresh start, in the trade publishing industry? It's hard enough to get publishers to catch up to the modern times, much less erase any slate and work from zero.

Pendel is swimming in the highs of another deal when Marina enters his office. "Hey Henry, congrats!" The assistant is looking for more advice, another agenting seminar. Pendel reads her enthusiasm as false, practiced, when it's more likely that Marina is the only person who can provide him with a genuine compliment without any contingencies attached. Still, Pendel takes it and defaults with, "What is it? What's the damage?"

She laughs, "For once we don't have any fires to put out. Actually, I have a certain editor you've been desperate to speak to on the line."

"Hendrix?"

She nods, "Yup. He offers his apology for being slow and unreachable."

"Of course," he says. "Impression is that I'm easily able to move on without him, evidenced by selling a debut for six figures to a nobody, a new editor on the scene. Hendrix can sense how easy it is to fall off my short list of exclusivities." Pendel gestures for the phone, Marina lowers her chin, signaling yes, he's waiting on line one. "He's probably in damage mode." He reaches for the phone, hand over the receiver, "Thank you Marina, you can go."

"Right," she says, hesitating a little before leaving the office.

Pendel's going to enjoy every minute of this conversation.

"Hendrix, what gutter did you crawl out of, hmm?"

"I deserve that," he says. "It's been brutal here. Our budget was cut in half. I can't acquire anything. We've got a tentative freeze, so even I can't pick up easy sells."

"Yeah, yeah, excuses," Pendel says, readying to pounce. "What you should really be explaining is how you plan on saving your career after you lose your biggest author."

"Pendel, I already said I'm sorry. The facts are there, we're in a freeze."

"Yeah well, if you can't buy Church now, you won't buy Church later. I'll go somewhere else. Come now, there's no limit. Someone will risk putting in an offer; it just takes having a spine."

Hendrix goes quiet.

"Did I scare you? Hendrix," Pendel gets down to brass tacks: "You and I have done business for years. This should be a done deal. I told you back when we first started that I'd elevate your career. Mine too. What have I done? I did that. I'm still doing that.

Here's your latest promotion and mark of prestige: J.D. Church's latest novel, *The Renegades*, in a *multi*-book deal. I'm thinking, hmm, oh, maybe a three-book deal so we don't have to keep doing this. You can cool off with all your manuscripts and I can move on to other matters."

"How much are we talking about?"

Pendel gets a calendar reminder. Brunch.

"Speak of the devil," Pendel chuckles. "I'm about to meet with our author right now. How about I bring him the perfect gift? Thinking to the sound of a seven-figure book deal."

Hendrix sighs, "I'll make it work."

"Good," Pendel says. "Circle back this afternoon. I'm out to lunch."

Chapter 12

Church's favorite spot for brunch is deep in Brooklyn. Black Swan isn't anything special, which is the reason why he likes it so much. When you're someone like Church, you got a lot to hide. Better to stick to the less popular and visible locales. I'm a little early, what a surprise, so I walk around the neighborhood in two and three-block circles, rotating around, keeping to a casual and common pace. It's just like Pendel to take a car, which I spot heading up Bedford Ave, windows down, Pendel living up the day. He just announced that book deal. Every single one counts. According to Publishers Marketplace, he's nearing the hundred mark on reported deals. Granted there are plenty that never make it onto the site, but he's not anybody.

For a person like Pendel, getting the deal announcement might be worth more than ensuring that the author attached even knows that a deal has been made.

Oh! Did I let something slip?

He'll figure it out, eventually. The media's got to catch on first.

Still got a bit of time. Just enough for him to pull up to Black Swan, step out, and give the neighborhood a scowl—yeah, you expect more; better accommodations—before stepping into the dark expanse of the faux-Irish pub.

I walk up and stand off to the side, setting a timer for 15

minutes. I reach into my jacket pocket. Rolled a joint, just for this occasion. Don't normally smoke, but every once in a while...

Mostly it's for the look.

Just another hipster in the hood. Meaning: completely ignored.

I'm giddy, like some child waiting in line for the latest video game. Takes me a minute to figure out why. He won't recognize me, not until I mention my name. But maybe I won't; rather, I'll pretend to be someone else. I'll be anybody as long as I get a feel for who he is.

On paper, he's extraordinary.

What's he like in person?

Timer screams. I put out the rest of the joint, feeling the dull pull of an incoming high.

Time to have a little fun.

Let's play.

Inside the restaurant, I walk past the bar immediately to my right and I make my way to the headwaiter, my story at the ready "Hey there, doing well, hope it's not too busy, well good, yeah, I'm here looking for a friend, tall guy, short black hair, I'm so bad with descriptions, sorry, yeah, well, oh I can go on ahead? Well thanks, thank you, I'm looking forward to the food."

Every story has its sides; sometimes you only get to hear one.

The place is pretty empty, only a few tables occupied. I've already practiced this interaction, conceivably how an actor gets into character; it's all in my head until I'm walking past Pendel's table, stopping short, turning on the balls of my feet, and playing this card: "Oh! Hey, are you..." Every story has its sides... Here you'll only get to hear mine. "Yeah! You're Henry Pendel, right? I saw you on a panel at the Brooklyn Book Fest a couple years back! It was so interesting, as an author myself. It inspired me to go on a deep dive online, reading the different business-of-publishing interviews that you did for *Writer's Digest,* and I've followed your manuscript wishlist too!" Pendel hasn't updated his wishlist since he wrote it. Likewise, most of his interviews were ghostwritten by his assistant. Someone like Pendel, he prides himself on being busy. Too busy. So what better way than to skip his discomfort, his mumbling, his tense body language, as I continue my storied performance?

"Actually, I'm working on a novel myself. It isn't done yet, I have a few chapters left, it's just that it's so hard to find the time to write when I'm working so many gigs to pay the rent, yeah you know how it is, the rent in this city, it's insane how anyone can afford it, and really I moved here to be a writer, to become inspired, to get involved in the literary community, you know, readings and workshops, you see I've been doing workshops, actually, I'm workshopping my novel right now, I've gotten so much good feedback, I'm ecstatic that people that have read it dig it, so this is like, the universe putting us together, huh? You just happening to be here, where I am all the time, never expected *the* Henry Pendel to show at a local haunt, it must be a sign!"

He keeps looking past me, like I'm not standing there.

Expecting... who else? J.D. Church.

Expectations aside, I expect him to call the server over for help. Waiting just long enough for discomfort to turn into anger, I see it switch over, and then I sit down, the confidence poised to make it appear as though I was the person he had been waiting for to arrive.

"Excuse me," he says. "I am flattered, and I wish you the best with your writing career, but what are you doing?"

"What, did I do something wrong?" I ask.

The server approaches, "Welcome! Can I start you on some drinks, water?"

He ignores the server, "Yes, you're invading my privacy and—"

"I'll have an old fashioned," I say, deflating the situation. "When it comes to alcohol," I pause, chuckling, "I guess I'm old-fashioned." More laughter. All mine.

Pendel is speechless.

"Sir," he says, between grit teeth. "If you don't honor my request to leave, I will have to resort to different matters."

"Were you waiting for someone?" I act confused. "Wow, holy fuck." I stand back up, ready to deliver the last of my side of the story: "I'm so damn sorry, I overstepped my boundaries, I was just so excited to see you, *in the flesh*, I got ahead of myself, but did you like what I said about my book? Would it be something maybe you'd like to see? Should I query you when it's ready? I'd love to, if you think it's of any interest to you."

His side remains erased, nonessential to the story being told.

Before leaving, I drop a bit of wisdom, "We all have a story to tell. Some are just willing to do anything to tell it."

"That's good," he says. "Put it in your book."

"Oh, I will," I say under my breath. If only he saw the blade at the center of that blurb; a threat perhaps of all that we have in store, him and I.

Was it fun? All I'd hoped?

You know, I'm not quite sure. When you anticipate something for so long, you kind of build it up into a fiction that cannot be contained in any sense of reality. I'm not really sure if it's disappointment or if I expected Pendel to put up more of a front, maybe a fight. Couldn't he have at least understood that it was me, Alex Moyer?

Well, one thing's for sure:

Pendel on the page and Pendel in person, they're exactly the same.

Chapter 13

New York Times bestseller and multiple-award winner of the Stoker, Legion, and Jackson awards **J.D. Church**'s **THE RENEGADES**, about a group of five survivors over the course of five pivotal climate-change events detailing the uprising of a new cross-dimensional civil war, in a major four-book deal, to **Hendrix de Leon** at **Alfred A. Wolf**, by **Henry Richmond Pendel** at **Cooper Willis Endeavor** (NA).

That's two for two. Two deals announced in two days. Pendel's on fire and he's not about to slow down now. The Church deal is the Deal of the Day and quickly makes the rounds across industry talking heads. On social media, fans are speculating about Church's slight genre shift from horror to something rooted more in mystery and science fiction. Talk of a cross-dimensional war has some confused, borderline worried, while other fans are excited to see something new from the popular author. Pendel's takeaway is that there's still a lot of money to be had from these big trade publishers. Even under the threat of sales and mergers, Alfred A. Wolf offered 8 million and a four-book deal. Frankly, Pendel thinks he could have gotten more, but chose to accept the deal with a better royalty rate, four installments instead of what would have been dozens across four books. What Hendrix doesn't realize is that Pendel demanded a clause in the contract that offers the possibility for renegotiation down the line.

Two for two.

He's got to keep this up.

"Marina," he shouts. "Get in here."

"Morning, Mr. Pendel," she says.

"You got the week's submission shortlist?" He gets right to business, "And see if you can get a hold of Church's wife, Becky."

"I have the list," she says. "It's already in your inbox! And sure thing. Is there a problem?"

Pendel comes up with an excuse, "I just need to discuss something. It's personal. Don't worry about it. Just get her on the line, okay?"

"Will do," she says. After she's gone, he turns to his inbox, scrolling through all the correspondence, people once again congratulating him on the Deal of the Day—the usual swarming of people seeking sub rights. Today is different. It could be that he's disappointed, or rather, it could be that subconsciously he understands that something's wrong with Church. Whatever it is, it keeps him from enjoying all the attention.

People are already asking about preorders. That's what you call a devoted readership.

He finds Marina's email and scrolls through the list. He still expects to see a name he recognizes, an author desperately looking to jump ship and sign with the best, but instead, it's a bunch of no-names. Debuts. On a second glance, one name pokes through.

Alexander Moyer.

"No fucking way," he whispers. "Marina!"

She pokes her head into the office, "Yes?"

"Umm, this one query by... Alexander Moyer, what, umm, jumped out to you?"

"Oh, it's a really cool concept!" She starts talking about the novel, identical in both premise and title as the previous query, the one they already passed on.

He interrupts, "You do realize he's already queried us."

"Oh, I didn't think he did... I thought I checked."

"He did," Pendel says, arms folded. "And we passed."

"Odd," she says. But unlike him, she sees it merely as a mistake, an oversight. "He will be stricken from the list."

"Yeah," Pendel says. "Umm, get Benji on the line."

"Right now?"

"Right now," he says.

He needs to update him on the new development. Benji isn't going to believe this. Yet when he's telling him about the repeat query, it doesn't get the lawyer nearly as concerned.

"It doesn't bother you?"

"Not really," says Benji. "It proves my point: He's obsessed. He's obsessed with becoming your author."

"Shouldn't this be filed away as new evidence?"

"We can," Benji says. "If you like."

Pendel searches for the author's name. There are several Alexander Moyers in the world, at least one being a semi-pro athlete. One Alexander is deceased. Really, all this does is make it difficult for Pendel to find anything on the guy. In fact, there's only one link, to a story newly published today. Moyer doesn't have any social media. The story is called "Survivors," and is published by a prominent literary journal called the *London Review*. Pendel listens to his lawyer's long-winded explanation about how there's still nothing else to be done here. This could violate the restraining order, a repeat query, yet it also involves having to reach out and interact with the stalker. "It's just not worth it at this point," Benji says. "The fact remains: He's yet another writer who sees you as the only choice for career success."

"And they'll do anything to tell their story..." Pendel murmurs, skim reading the story.

"Huh? Yeah, sure," Benji says. "Again, like I said before, keep track of everything and be sure to forward this query to me so that I have it too. I'll put it with the rest."

"Yeah," he says.

"Anything else?"

Pendel doesn't hear him. The truth hits hard; this Alexander Moyer, he's a good writer. The story is about a group of survivors stuck in the battlefields of war. It delves into speculative fiction when it's revealed that the war is multi-dimensional and that the war is being waged over control of the remaining inhabitable lands on Earth. Pendel reads it and fails to see the glaring coincidence.

"Henry? You okay?"

He clears his throat, "Yeah. Yeah." He can't stop reading the story.

"We'll be in touch," Benji says and hangs up.

Marina reenters his office, all color flushed from her face. Her lip quivers, "Mr. Pendel..."

"What is it, Marina? Can't you see I'm reading?"

The story grips him enough that in the back of his mind, he almost wants to look at the full manuscript. He doesn't notice how upset his assistant is, nor does he see the swift and sudden shift in the sorts of emails arriving in his inbox. From congratulatory to caustic, the subject lines tell a horrific story, one of bad timing and a future unimaginable. And Pendel's going to be caught in the middle of it.

"Mr. Pendel," she says, nearly shouting.

He looks up from the computer screen, "What?!"

"J.D. Church was found dead."

Chapter 14

Same day you announce a lucrative deal, the author turns up dead. Ouch, talk about bad luck. That's the kind of thing that changes a person. What's a literary agent to do? He's having the worst day of his life. I'm having a good day, was able to bear witness to the discovery.

And I got published! You'd think I'd feel a certain way about plagiarism, but I changed it enough to make it my own. Truth is, I made it better. Things *happen* in my story. After trimming all the fat, I was left with 7k words. Just enough to wow the editors at the *London Review*. They got back to me the same day. Feels nice, being seen and successful. Guess that's why Church lost his mind. You let it get to your head, become power-hungry, demanding validation from everyone, all hours of the day and night. You want it all, and when you have it, you want something you can never have.

He wanted to feel alive. *Alive,* something he'll never have again.

Don't know what you got until it's gone.

I'm just another hotel guest when housekeeping finds Church's body in the tub, the liquid less water and more chemicals and blood. His body has already begun to decompose, just enough that it makes first sight an instant horror. At least one of those employees will quit on the spot and for that, I must apologize. It's the only part I'll apologize for, those that are too close and get hit by shrapnel. Occupational hazard. They find the body and I hear both women scream from my room. I'm one of five hotel guests loitering in the hallway, already a security guard has begun controlling the scene of the crime.

"What happened?"

"Oh my god..."

"Someone died!"

The clatter of onlookers quickly realizing the severity of the situation. I play along, even shedding a few tears when the cops arrive.

"How could something like this happen?!"

That one is me, thank you. Even get one of the cops to talk to me, offering a hug. He tells me what I already know, which is much more than a cop should tell any bystander. It's the author, a famous author. Dead. Looks like it might have been suicide.

The last part is a lie, but this early they still haven't found the pages tucked away for safekeeping under his skin. They don't see the notes I gave, the result of a productive workshop. Instead, there's a lot of mitigating the sanctity of the scene. Eventually, we'll be told to leave the scene, that we're intruding, and the age-old "nothing to see here!"

Oh, but there's plenty to see.

Media will get their hands on the details a little over an hour later. The worst of the worst, places like TMZ, will cover the story. For most any other author, it would remain in literary circles, most likely on social media, but for a big name like J.D. Church, it gets celebrity treatment.

His story matters to many.

The shock that reverberates across the media when details leak about how they found pages *inside of the body* will get people talking, though I don't see how it's any more shocking than the snoozefest of his novel and how it landed him millions.

What about Pendel... how does he find out?

I've always had an overactive imagination, which works well for my career path. I can imagine his side of the story, how he finds out, and how it's deliberate, the part about finding out after everyone else. Pendel's too self-absorbed to care about the well-being of his authors.

Here's what'll happen, no doubt:

The media spreads the news like a virus. The one most likely to deliver the news is a colleague, likely his assistant, Marina Grace. He'll be in the middle of basking in being the man behind today's Deal of the Day, probably already onto another deal, selling the rights to the book, maybe already talking about turning it into a movie. Same as always, he is a jackal, cutthroat and thinking only about the next deal. That's where the news will find him, and that's how I will see him backed into a corner, one that he won't see until it's already too late. Journalists will be quick to hit him up for a quote. There'll be emails in his inbox swarming, and then Pendel will hear from his editor, and then it'll be a frenzy of battling what the media gets and what they decide to say. Pendel walks into a living nightmare.

But at least it'll be lucrative.

Never mind that there is no manuscript. There will never be any manuscript with the title *The Renegades* and no new words from J.D. Church. The deal made is a deal that will inevitably be a blunder, one lost. Never mind that he doesn't think of it, not yet. Never mind that he doesn't think about where, and how, the media and Church's readership will position him. Never mind the late-night drunk texts with the author mere hours before his death. Never mind that he doesn't put any of the pieces together, doesn't even realize that there's a puzzle in need of solving.

Whatever's left of the manuscript is now evidence. The editors there said they devoured it; they simply couldn't look away. That's how I want people to react to my body of work.

When I do something, they can't look away.

It's the biggest compliment any author can get.

It's what I aspire to do, and by the way they're reacting to Church's death, already talking about it being the work of a *serial killer*, it seems my process is working! They already want a sequel. No, they expect a sequel. Well, lucky for them, I'm thinking bigger picture; an entire industry to encompass. I think many will join me in this story.

What comes to mind is identical to the reason it had to be Church. Same reason it'll put the rest of his authors in danger. I'm building a body of work; he's going to build an empire, fully funded off the posthumous financial boons of every dead author on his list. All he needs to do is reply. Listen to me. I'll be your highest-selling author.

When that assistant of his relays the news, he doesn't burst into tears; he doesn't fall apart. No, that's not like Pendel at all. Once he hears the news, he thinks, *I'm going to squeeze another couple million out of Hendrix.*

Part Two
EMERGING AUTHOR

Chapter 1

J.D. Church is trending across social media. TMZ broke the news first, followed by *The New York Times*. Soon it's on everyone's mind, and users all have their own sorrow-ridden posts reaching for maximum engagement. Everyone wants to be involved in the media spotlight of a sudden and unfortunate death. A few of Pendel's clients are quick to comment on the breaking news, including his recent deal-winner, Brendon Kawada, and long-time client, Mallory McAllister.

I'm shocked. I just don't know what to say. A big loss to the world of letters. Kawada follows up the post with a thread listing out his favorite books, stories, and interviews Church published *during his lifetime.* His thread goes viral alongside many others. McAllister's post is even more emotional. *I am glad to have been able to know and adore J.D. Church. He was a kind and complicated soul. I'm in tatters here; I don't know how to go on.* What follows is a customary ticker tape of condolences from hundreds of followers.

Pendel sifts through social media but remains quiet, unable to post anything for himself. People DM and message him across all channels, offering their condolences. A few reporters have reached out for a quote, something to add to their own *breaking news* content. Pendel is beside himself, stricken by what can only be described as the *worst timing ever.*

Then the agency sends someone to his office and suddenly silence and solitude become impossible. It isn't a grief counselor; rather, Pendel's talking to an employee with the agency that he hasn't met before. His name is Mauro or Michael or Marcus. He doesn't quite remember; Pendel's been told that this guy is in the agency's internal communications department and specializes in crisis mitigation and prevention.

"You're going to want to issue a statement. The investigation underway will likely make it to us, and we at CWE will have to say something. We should get ahead of it and send a press release to the media."

"Okay," Pendel says, not quite paying attention. He continues to stare at social media, giving himself to the infinite scroll of the timeline.

"I can get started, if you like."

The guy is all business, which normally Pendel would find to be an endearing quality, a positive character trait, but something's on his mind. It isn't Church's death, or all that's going to inevitably land on his desk, the good, bad, and ugly. It's something far deeper. The source of the bother is that Pendel has no means to process the depth of this feeling.

His skill set has always specialized in pushing things away, ignoring the problem, parlaying it with productivity. That's not going to work, not this time. So what else is left? Nothing, except the feeling he simply cannot shake, the feeling that renders him foggy, unable to fully be anywhere. Lost to the infinite spiral of unprocessed thoughts.

"You'll want to put something personal in the press release," he says. "You've been his agent for 12 years; it might be good to offer some candor, highlighting Church's work ethic, his unstoppable, meteoric rise to literary fame. There was nobody else but you who experienced it as close to first-hand as Church."

"Yeah," Pendel says.

Marina walks into the office, "Sorry, but umm..."

"It's okay," the guy says, whatever his name is, "We're basically done here." He stands up from his seat and gives his goodbyes, "Expect the draft within the half hour."

When the guy is gone, Pendel is still, no telling when he'll stop, scrolling through the endless posts about Church's death.

"Becky's on line two," Marina says.

That'll work, snapping him back to the situation at hand. "Oh," Pendel stutters. "We—well, then, umm, thank you?"

"Sure," Marina says. Nothing is okay. Not right now. She hangs her head, keeping every motion and murmur to a solemnity that can only be translated as mourning. There is no other way to react.

He picks up the phone, Becky already in tears, hysterical on the other line, "Hi there Becky. My condolences."

"What the hell are condolences going to do?! What are we going to do?! He's dead! He's fucking dead!!"

Pendel listens to Church's wife, newly a widow, rant about how she thinks it was due to all the allegations, the negative media spin over the last couple of months. She's almost incoherent when she talks about an internal investigation at the university, something Pendel hadn't been aware of, and after a few minutes of pure anger, Becky defaults to sorrow.

"I don't know what to do. How do I continue without him?"

"I'm so sorry," Pendel says. He never apologizes, yet under the circumstances, there's always a possibility for a first.

"This isn't like the movies," she says. "There is no clear act of vengeance. Someone doesn't pay for his death."

Well, actually...

Pendel grins, then offers her some solace, "Oh on the contrary. Jerry was my author. It's my responsibility to ensure that his work, and his name, lives on through a lucrative, very lucrative, legacy."

Becky perks up, "What are you saying?"

"I'm saying that deal we just made, it's looking like we're going to quadruple it."

Money talks. In the case of Church, money has the propensity to heal. You can hear it in how quickly she calms down, the cocktail of intense emotion downgraded to a low whisper, something that she'll carry in as much grief can be carried.

"Tell me more," she says.

"I will, once I make a few moves," he says.

Without any way of processing the loss, Pendel turns to productivity.

"Some homework for you, maybe it'll even help keep your mind off things."

Becky can be heard sobbing, "That would be good."

"Dig up all of Jerry's unpublished writings. Everything, even if it's letters, reviews, anything."

"Okay..."

"It's time to gather ammunition for a big sale."

Hearing Church's widower finding hope through a big payday only sweetens the opportunity. And it is an opportunity.

A big one. Becky will know more soon. It's time to make that call.

Hendrix picks up the phone and says, "Henry. Jesus, man. How are you faring? Are you okay? I just can't believe it."

"There's a lot that's unbelievable right now," says Pendel. "For instance, I can't believe how big of an opportunity we have, you and me. We may have lost our author, but he's given us a license to print money."

"I'm listening," he says.

Chapter 2

I've always liked going to literary readings. Never really made a lot of sense to me why so many authors speak ill of this sort of event, like the occasion to read your own work and hear the work of others, maybe compare notes and techniques, was something deemed *lesser* by the literary elite. You don't have to do events or give readings if you're a *big enough* author. That's the impression, but really, when you go to the right readings, you tend to notice that some of the biggest names headline those reading series. Hell, often they are the ones running them!

As a newly published author, I figure I should go to the reading.

This series has been ongoing for nearly eight years. The Metropolitan Ave Lit Series, that's what it's called. My story goes something like, "Oh I'm new to all this. Just got my first story published! The *London Review*! I know, I'm ecstatic! Thank you so much! I'm just happy to be here!" Really, I've already planned out my attendance. There'll be someone who is a no-show—the person opening the reading. Turns out he ends up with food poisoning. I wonder how that happened. He ate some Vietnamese the other night. That place on Franklin Ave. Their pho is to die for. He almost did. Maybe we crossed paths, and maybe we "compared notes."

He recently celebrated a publication too. I saw it all over his social media. It's so easy to figure out where an author lives, what an author's up to, and most of all, what an author is going through, thanks to some idea that became industry gospel, the *need* to put yourself out there if you want to be an author; if you aren't broadcasting and documenting every detail of your life, people won't care about your story. Anyway, I have my story, and he has his; the difference is that I'll get to talking with the curator of the series after she finds out he's sick.

Right place and the right time.

She's cursing under her breath, talking to one of the other authors when I step forward, invisible in the crowd up until now. Start with some compliments, and then allow the topic to cut through. Play up the problem, and then, when the time is right, chime in with the story.

"Just got my first story published!"

"Congrats! Where can I find it?" She's practiced this response. Can't imagine how many authors have talked about their publications, with her at the receiving end. She feigns interest until hearing who published it.

"The *London Review*!"

"Wow, congratulations!" This time she's sincere. "That's amazing."

"I know, I'm ecstatic!"

And then it's right there, low-hanging fruit.

"Did you maybe want to read from it?" She offers before she's fully certain that she should, but it's because I'm so charming that she leans into it, preferring the easy solution to her latest predicament. "I know it's putting you on the spot but—"

"I'd love to!"

Beautiful. Plays itself out perfectly. The readers sit in a VIP area, a booth in the back corner, away from the crowd. That's where I see her for the first time, the author Chelsea Boll. She's an emerging author, with a few novellas published with indie presses, and what looks to be a major debut novel being positioned by—who else?—Henry Richmond Pendel. She's sitting with the other authors, silent and evidently nervous.

The other authors chat, industry talk and the usual narrow range of topics:

"Yeah, should have it done in time for the deadline my agent gave me..."

"Teaching at CUNY and also building out a private workshop."

"He got a six-figure advance, but I bet he isn't going to earn out."

"Publishing is an addiction. You can never get enough."

I'm sitting across from her, and when I lean forward and whisper the words, "Hey, big fan!" She grins and says thanks. It seems genuine enough. "The story you published in the *Human Monsters* anthology was amazing, just a masterful piece of psychological horror."

Validation is an author's kryptonite. Give them something sincere and one-sided, and they'll reveal their hand. When everything is so transactional, something genuine comes along and it becomes my perfect murder weapon.

All I need to do is treat an author like a human being. Show some compassion, and it all falls into place.

"You actually read that story?"

I nod, "I did."

"Thanks. Didn't think anybody actually read my stuff. It's all on tiny, indie presses."

"Someone's always reading," I say. A compliment, a threat. I know all about her. Chelsea Boll. Beyond her publications, she is like seemingly everybody else: a New York City transplant. Three years in the city, she lives a solitary life. She graduated with an MFA from the Iowa Writers Workshop, which is no small feat. It opened doors, got Pendel's attention, and it soon gave her ins with a lot of unreachable editors of different publications. Yet she suffered from writer's block, and not just any bout of writer's block, the kind where she couldn't write what was pitched or assigned. All she could write was experimental horror, stories that lacked plot and favored imagery and mood. She was relegated to the small and indie press world, and her peers, people in her cohort at Iowa Writers Workshop, all started to cut her loose. No more invitations to their writing group, no more invitations to the weekly dinner party and cocktail hour. She was cut loose and in doing so, she felt the sting of nonacceptance.

The curator addresses the table, "Alright, here's the lineup..."

I go first, followed by two other authors, a 15-minute break, followed by Boll and then the curator. Everyone says they're fine with the lineup. The moment she leaves, there are whispers about her interjecting herself as the headliner.

"Does she always do that?"

"Yeah, that's normal."

"Isn't that... like, you know, kind of shameless?"

Authors judging other authors. My attention is directed exclusively to Boll, who continues to stay out of the conversation, withdrawn for reasons that have everything to do with carrying trauma about not being accepted by a literary community.

"You're going to kill it," I tell her.

"Maybe that's what I need to do," she forces a laugh.

"Maybe you're right," I wink.

I spot her blushing a little, unintentional flattery, but it's all part of the story. Like, if my reading goes well. I go up there with enough confidence and imagine myself reading to a group of people who actually care. Short intro and I'm reading eight minutes of "Survivors." Applause afterward, and a few of the authors at the table tell me, "Dude, that was amazing," and "Nice job."

But it's when Boll rests her hand on my forearm and says, "That was wonderful," then I know I've succeeded. Everything else is smooth sailing. Boll mumbles through her intro, which comes off as cute and endearing, though the authors at the table sigh, rolling their eyes, judging her elongated and slightly confusing explanation of the excerpt from her novel.

She reads for 12 minutes and the passage is striking, a horror that predicts her own bitter end. I take notes in advance of our late-night workshop. In the passage, the young woman is seduced and led to the man's apartment where he slips her a roofie. The guy reveals his true intentions, her long lost brother, and proceeds to torture and maim her, revenge for taking "his place" in the family.

He talks about how her birth was an accident, and that her mother and father used her as a stopgap when he went missing.

Her excerpt goes over well; the audience applause is delayed, everyone in shock by the graphic detail of the mutilation scenes. I'm the lone person who claps, later joined by others.

"That's from your novel?" I say, when she's back at the table. Note that she sits next to me rather than across.

"Yeah!"

She's relieved, enjoying the high of those post-reading minutes.

"Absolutely harrowing," I say.

The curator takes the stage. All throughout the rest of the readers, I'm chatting up Boll, whispers traded about where she got the idea for her novel, the process of writing it, and how in many ways she channeled her own trauma into the story.

When the reading concludes, people stick around and order drinks. Books are for sale up at the front of the venue. A line forms around one of the authors, the name doesn't matter. Only Boll, she's my focus, *my author*.

We remain alone at the VIP table.

After some awkward silence, me getting a chance to take in her aura, thinking about how the rest of the night will unfold, I ask her, "Up for getting a nightcap somewhere?"

"It's like you read my mind," she grins.

"Yeah, this sucks. Let's get out of here."

The best part of going anywhere is being able to leave.

Chapter 3

Pendel isn't offering a pitch; it's an ultimatum. Positioning Hendrix in yet another compromised situation, it's evident in how Hendrix doesn't bother with negotiations. This has happened before. It's a ticking clock; the news of an author's death has a shelf life, and yet with an author like J.D. Church, there's the issue of where those posthumous releases will go. It doesn't necessarily retain exclusivity with Alfred A. Wolf just because Hendrix has been Church's editor for years. The hesitation is held against the editor, Pendel using the situation to get back at his editor. It has everything to do with spite.

"Tick tock, the entirety of J.D. Church's estate up for grabs," he says.

This has everything to do with the dry spell, that month of silence from Hendrix and the publisher; an entire month of ghosting Pendel. You don't do something like that, especially when you've worked closely to build one of the biggest authors and brands in modern history.

To say that Church is an institution is an understatement.

"What do you want?" Hendrix asks, and then immediately corrects himself, "What do you need from me?"

"Some assurance," Pendel says. "Rather, some insurance." He offers a warning, "You're going to miss him when he's gone."

"Insurance...?"

"I need a gesture of good faith. Think of his widower. Becky's lost the love of her life and the main source of income. Surely all the success of the past will sustain her and their kids, but how can we be so sure, especially in this day and age?"

Hendrix listens intently, dreading Pendel's next demand.

"I'm thinking about renegotiating the current deal," he offers, sticking it to him. "Why stop at a four-book deal when it can be an exclusive, a full exclusive of every unpublished work to Church's name? It's all up for grabs." The blade's sharp, and he can hear it in Hendrix's voice, a rattle in every syllable that proves to Pendel that he has the editor on his heels.

"You say that, but we did already come to a deal for *The Renegades* and his most recent work," Hendrix says.

Turn and twist the blade, "But we didn't sign the contract. Not yet."

Boom, silence. Hendrix is stunned. There's an audible sigh, followed by Hendrix waving the white flag in defeat, "Okay. Tell me what you want, and I'll make it happen."

"You will make it happen, won't you?"

A knock at the door.

Expecting to see Marina yet again with another question, instead he sees a man with short graying hair, a blazer, and a dress shirt without a tie. He offers a wave, "Hi there, Mr. Pendel? Your assistant let me through."

"Yeah, and you are?"

"Detective Monroe. Mitchell Monroe. Is now a good time?"

A knot forms in Pendel's gut, a series of half-thoughts form—tell him you're grieving, tell him you're in the middle of inking an important deal, tell him you're about to be in another meeting—and then abandon him before they can become in any way logical and legit. They're all bad ideas, and inevitably, Pendel has no choice but to give the detective his attention.

"Hendrix, I'll call you back," Pendel says, ending the call. "Please," he gestures to the chair on the other side of his desk. "Have a seat."

"Thank you," says the detective.

Pendel reads the detective's body language as he strolls over to the seat, lowers himself, and crosses his legs. The dirt and scuffs on his shoes, the wrinkled shirt, the sight of it all bothers Pendel, leaving him even more on edge than usual.

The edge, it comes from the fact that, well, Pendel simply isn't that upset about his author's demise. In death, his author will be as lucrative, if not *more* lucrative, than he was when alive and well. At the very least, it keeps all the allegations and other negative publicity at bay. For a little bit. It'll bite back, but it gives the agency communications department, as well as Benji, more time to form a strategic plan of defense. If it comes to it, they'll be ready to attack.

"Would you like anything to drink?" Pendel asks.

"No thank you," says Monroe. He takes out an equally worn notepad and pen, like something out of a film noir story. "Just have a few questions. It shouldn't take up too much of your time."

"Are you sure? I can always get you something to drink," Pendel says.

Detective Monroe narrows his gaze, "Just a few questions. If that's okay?"

That tone just now, Pendel leans forward, elbows on his desk, "Sure, sure, whatever you need. My sincerest apologies if I'm a little scattered. A lot has happened."

The detective chuckles, "You could say that again. Oh! What am I thinking? Please, my condolences. Seems my mind is elsewhere too."

"Not at all," says Pendel.

The empty space between action and response is enough for Pendel to lose his cool. Just come out with it already. Yet the detective lets him sweat a little, perhaps fully aware of how uncomfortable of an encounter this is for someone who hadn't foreseen its occurrence.

"So, the questions? I'm all ears," says Pendel.

"Mmhmm," the detective says, reviewing his notes. "Just one second..."

"Sure thing," he says, leaning back in his chair, hands folded.

"Okay," the detective clicks his pen, "How long have you been J.D. Church's agent?"

He leans forward, "12 years. 12 great, highly productive years."

"And were you two close? What was the nature of your interactions?"

"It was... professional. We often exchanged banter about the industry, but outside of Jerry updating me about his work, we kept things fairly cordial."

The hesitation there, a detective notes something like that. "And you just finalized another book deal, correct?"

"Oh yes, a great one. One that would have sustained him for many years of creativity and future success. But now it'll have to be only in memory. I'm way ahead on ensuring that his work and his intellectual property will live on without him."

"Great. Great," the detective jots something down. "Is this the deal with Alfred A. Wolf?"

"It could be. I'm waiting on another offer. I'm thinking it needs to be more than four books."

"I see," the detective cocks his head to one side. "Hmm, actually, perhaps you might be able to clear something up."

"Sure," Pendel says.

"There was a second deal?"

"Not exactly."

"You see where I'm not following, right?"

"I'm actively working on an entirely different deal."

"And this was before or after Mr. Church's passing?"

Pendel puts it all together. This looks bad.

"After."

The floor shakes, Pendel's leg tapping rapidly, a nervous tell that both he and the detective spot at the same time.

"Anyway," Pendel says, hoping to change the subject. "I'm always looking out for my authors. Sometimes you just got to focus on what you can control."

"Yes..." Detective Monroe writes in his notepad, Pendel watching nervously.

"Was there anything else?"

Monroe clicks his pen, "We can put a bookmark in it. For now."

"Excellent," Pendel grins. He stands up and offers his hand, "Thank you for dropping by." Don't forget to show empathy. "And for, umm, what's the word... the condolences."

The detective shakes his hand, "We'll be in touch."

We'll be in touch. The detective leaves behind a sobering revelation, to even the inexperienced inquisitor, Pendel didn't look even remotely upset about his client's passing.

This is only the beginning.

Chapter 4

Nightcap at some bar called Moot, just the two of us, the trajectory of both our conversation and inevitable commingling being in and of itself moot. She isn't used to being treated nicely, which is unfortunately more commonplace than it should be. People are looking for a story to relate to, a narrative where they can experience a happy moment or two, maybe even a happy ending.

One drink becomes three, and I'm the one buying.

She's doing all the talking.

"You wrote the novel in three weeks!"

"I did," she says, before taking another sip.

"So what's keeping you from getting that big time book deal?"

She looks at me, this look of defeat, and downs the rest of her drink.

"You can tell me," I say. "I don't know anything about this industry. I'm a nobody."

"You got published in the *London Review*," she says. "Well on your way."

"Maybe." My turn to nurse the drink.

Boll needs that extra push, the undeniable feeling that she is with a trusted person, someone who has no reason to hold anything against her, and to feel like she can speak her mind.

She sighs, "I get it. I get the feeling of being vulnerable because you feel like nobody really cares, and that it's an uphill battle, trying to be read and published."

"I know you get it," I tell her. But what I'm really waiting for is her confession. There's a reason why she still hasn't gotten her book deal, and I'm two steps ahead. I know why. She just needs to say it and then we can go from there.

Out in the open, ready to take it in stride, "You don't have to tell me. It's okay."

"I'll tell you," she says. Reverse psychology, the tried and true, it always seems to yield the truth. "I don't think I'm a priority."

"Priority?"

"Yeah, my agent signed me, and he was there, very responsive at first; then a few weeks go by, I'm finished with his edits for the manuscript, and then it takes three days and an email nudge to get a response. He tells me that somehow the email slipped by and that he's sorry and can't wait to read the new revision."

"Ugh, that sucks," I say. Pendel's MO. But I'm not supposed to know the identity of her agent. Not until she's told me.

She keeps going, "I circle back with him after a month, feeling like that's a good enough amount of time for an agent to read it, right?"

"Right."

"And he takes a few days to get back to me and it's some terse email saying, I have feedback for you. He doesn't say what or when, and then it takes me prying via successive emails to see that he might have ideas for yet another revision."

"The doldrums," I say.

"Right but he hasn't given me the feedback, the ideas, or whatever. I'm not a priority. The book could be out on submission, but he hasn't got around to me."

What I could say is that agents are busy. That's true. What I could say is that Pendel isn't every agent. That's also true. What I could also say is that Pendel's really good at his job because he cares only about the dollar signs and major deals, and that would be, like everything else, true. Instead, I tell her what she wants to hear: "You deserve better, Chelsea."

"Yeah." She thinks about it and then says, "You're right."

She needed to let it out.

"I feel better," she grins.

"Nothing's worse than feeling like the person who should be your champion proves that they don't really care."

"Yeah," she says, eying the empty glass.

"I'll get us another round!"

"No," she says. "You've already paid for..."

I stand my ground, "No, I insist."

Chelsea, dear vulnerable Chelsea, you have no reason to worry. We're going to workshop every part of how this story ends.

After the third round, she's noticeably buzzed and I'm hiding my excitement. There are two ways the story could unfold, and I've planned for both. Yet she makes the selection with ease, "My apartment's like four blocks from here."

Boll is so starved for attention that she doesn't want our little flirtatious and fortuitous encounter to end. And why would she? I'm offering to read more of her manuscript, give her some feedback, Pendel's feedback that remains unsent.

I'll do anything for another author. I'll cut them open and find the power of their voice, the uniqueness of their own narrative. Like any laceration, an author's work bleeds out through every lived experience, just as every lived experience becomes a new vein from which the blood may flow. What it comes down to is being willing, open to another fresh wound.

Boll isn't like J.D. Church. She remains vulnerable, willing to be seen. She wants to tell her story. I'm going to find out if she's willing to do anything to tell it.

We spend the next hour on her couch, a printout of her novel, *Inside*, passed between us. She nods off occasionally, and I take those opportunities to get my tools, the entire process prepped and ready. Thankfully, I can keep everything I need in my little handy bag. None the wiser, I have the blade in one hand and a vial in another. The alcohol does most of the work, but there's still that extra push, the full reveal to get this workshop started.

"Chelsea," I say, waking her up. "Chelsea, I finished reading the chapter."

"You did..." She grins. "I'm so embarrassed. It's bad." Her eyelids remain shut, "It's really bad. My agent doesn't care because it's bad and he regrets signing me."

"Not true," I say. "Absolutely false."

I take her left arm, pinch the soft flesh of her wrist, just a little test, and then search for a vein, one good enough for this little jump start.

"I read the chapter; don't you want to hear what I think?"

Her mouth hangs open, voice barely audible, "I do..."

"Well then let's get started," I say, blade raised, sharpened and ready for her prose.

Chapter 5

Pendel doesn't know what to do with himself, so he turns to the easiest target in his proximity: Hendrix. It starts with an email, subject line: "Well?" in the email, he reiterates how easily the J.D. Church estate can exchange hands, become the cash cow of a competitor. There's so much at stake, and Pendel at least has this in his control. Doesn't even take that long to get a response, an email reply with Hendrix keeping it brief, "In a meeting with the publisher as I type this. Will know more soon."

Yeah, no. That's just not good enough.

Pendel starts making some calls to other editors. First up is what's-her-name. The editor at FSG. He uses the fresh Kawada deal and the fact that she had wanted the latest Church novel in the first place as leverage.

"Hey there," Pendel says. "Remember what I said about how that deal was only the beginning?"

She's nervous, you can hear it in her voice. "Yeah. I remember."

"I'm sure you've heard by now," Pendel says. He needs to be sure that he sounds grief-stricken, at least enough to potentially tap into her sympathies. The freshness of Church's death will potentially draw out every editor, not one with any pushback. Everyone's going to listen, and everyone's going to give in.

"I'm so sorry," she says.

Yeah, he doesn't actually care. There's no use for her apologies. Instead, he takes her half step and offers a full stride: "This is the call. The one that will make or break your career. You wanted the latest Church, well I'm offering you the latest and the last, every single unpublished manuscript."

She's speechless. Throat clearing followed by a jittery mess of a reply, "Then, uhh, so."

"Listen up. I said *listen up*. I always keep my word. Now's the chance, the moment where I hold out my hand and all you need to do is take it."

"But I was under the impression that a deal had already been made," she says.

These young editors, he just can't with them. "Hey, my hand. You got a narrow window to make an offer." He makes it even clearer, telling her that she has at best a half hour. "About as long as it takes me to call up other editors."

Before she can say anything else, he's ended the call and dials yet another editor. This guy, Pendel has always been bad with names, especially names attached to people from which he sees little value or people he dislikes, and this is no different. He's that senior editor at Macmillan. The guy always lowballs Pendel. He thinks the guy is a mediocre editor; just not that good at his job. Really, it's more like the editor doesn't play into Pendel's games. He doesn't find it of any use or interest attempting to clamor over Pendel's manipulative dealings, particularly when the agent pits editors against each other, provoking the biggest offer, peddling lies and other shadow play, in order to ensure that things fall in Pendel's favor. They have a history of disagreement, yet Pendel still calls him up.

"You probably have already heard," Pendel says.

"Yeah, how unfortunate. He was your best author," says the editor.

What a piece of shit. Pendel ignores the comment, "Now's your chance."

No need to spell it out, this editor's been around. "Thought Wolf had him on lock."

"Nothing's official until it's signed on the dotted line."

The editor thinks about it, pure silence on the line, each anguished second sending Pendel's stress level ever close to its peak, and then the editor says, "When do you need an offer?"

"Now," says Pendel.

"Can't do that," the editor says.

"Now meaning within the hour."

"How about 'Now meaning EOD?'"

Pendel sighs, "Just get me an offer quick."

Laughter on the other line as he ends the call.

He turns his attention back to his primary subject. Hendrix hasn't emailed back, but that's okay because here's Pendel with another update.

Update: "Seems there's interest."

Maybe one more call, just in case. Pendel thinks of that other editor, someone he's never worked with, but got close, once. She specializes in genre stuff, which works for J.D. Church, though really, category doesn't matter here. Church is a category all his own. Is, was, whatever.

Pendel's mid-sentence when she answers, "...just completely gutted. But I must do right for Jerry, and he deserves the best editor, publisher, and champion. With him gone, I need to know that his words are in trustworthy hands."

She starts with her condolences, and proceeds to go a full step further, "Reading J.D. Church's fiction helped me discover the joy of reading. I wouldn't be where I am if I hadn't read his novels. They opened an entire world. He's changed lives. Made a big difference. The book sales are one thing, but the way I see it, he's one of the reasons younger generations find their way to fiction. Look at any bookstore, he takes up multiple shelves."

Character details. Proof of her fandom. She's a long-time reader, hopeful new editor for the author. Pendel brushes it all aside, "Then you understand the importance of finding a champion befitting of his legacy."

"Yes," she says.

"I'll expect an offer within the hour."

"Wow, wait what?"

"You said it yourself, he's changed lives. Don't you want to be at the helm of ensuring that future generations may find and enjoy his work?"

She begins explaining the difficulty, the absolutely unrealistic sense of urgency Pendel is placing on the submission, but he cuts her off, "One hour."

He prods Hendrix with yet another update: "Seems they're willing to settle with the agency demands."

That's three other editors, cold-called and given a bargain, an offer that should be fathomed as once in a lifetime.

Basically, who wants to future-proof their career today?

Of course, even after all of this, the bitter aftertaste remains, and worse, he hasn't stopped thinking about the detective. We'll be in touch. What to do, what can he do? Nothing, and that gets him emailing a few other editors, none of whom he considered to be capable of a lucrative offer. But it's something. It keeps him busy.

Yet another update to Hendrix: "Going to be a big deal, Church heads to FSG!"

Pendel emails back and forth with editors. Whenever there's a lull, he returns to previous correspondence with Hendrix, reading between the lines, looking for something that isn't there. Could be that he's getting a little paranoid.

From one editor to another, they start talking about the impending acquisition, who will make the offer and who will live to regret it. And there's Pendel in wait, ready to bask in what could become a potential bidding war, one that will conclude with yet another career highlight.

All it took was having one of his authors pass away.

Chapter 6

Here's what I think about *Inside.* Chelsea does a wonderful job using the metaphor of bodily intrusion to explore the trauma of repeated sexual abuse from a sibling. The manuscript is 58 chapters long, yet really, the source of the story can be trimmed down to about half that number. Here's a story that is so internalized that every word is clearly that of the protagonist's thoughts, even when the details are externalized. She is a mailperson living a lonely existence; her friends all work at the post office and talk about her behind her back. This person she meets, her physical and mental identical, harbors a secret. From that excerpt she read at the literary reading, it was clear long before she let me inside who or what this antagonistic character symbolized.

"He did this to you, didn't he?"

That's okay, she doesn't need to say anything. Go ahead and ride that high, be lost to the unconscious web of dream and memory. I can take it from here. Some stories need a doctor, and surely, this is going to be exciting for me. A new experience, especially after the disappointment that was J.D. Church. These pages I cut from her story, they're nonessential. What remains is a lean 200 pages of hurt, and hell, the insides of a person splayed across a story that I now take, with great care, to tell externally.

"You know, he could have done more than just penetrate her," I say. "Sex is so blasé. He turns out to be her brother, which adds a notch of discomfort. Incest plus rape is pretty much the worst that can befall a person. But you see where things could shift and become far more menacing and effective, it's where the idea of 'inside' takes on another level."

The pages worth keeping are methodically arranged across the floor, her body stripped bare lays there, arms and legs stretched out among her work.

"To make it a lasting work, it must go beyond the body. It must penetrate the mind."

My workshopping should help. She's going to be a great addition to my body of work. It's up to me to make it worth it for her. If her life must end here, at least allow her story to lengthen as a tragedy across time itself.

I kneel next to her chest, her pale skin, ribcage visible, and I whisper, "Your story will be worth telling."

Never mind the pages I cut. They go in a metal trash bin. I take them into the bathroom, her tiny little studio apartment smelling of smoke after they are done away with. The smoke detector never sounds, agreeable with the events unfolding.

I look between her legs, and then again at her breasts. In most stories, these would be touched, adored, violated. I take special interest in her vagina, completely shaved, the slightest blemish on the lips is an indication of the real brother, the real abuse.

Where's my knife?

"Ah yes," I say, finding it resting on the sofa. "Inside. To get inside, it isn't about taking this," I raise the blade, "and inserting it into that," I point at the area between her legs. There's a need to make it clear, illustrate what I'm talking about. The blade won't fit all the way. It only goes a few inches deep, the blood pools around my wrist.

"Sometimes you just have to get your hands dirty," I say, chuckling. A single thrust, nothing more, and I let go. The knife remains inserted. By now, she shouldn't feel a thing. The dose flowing through her veins will take her somewhere close, slowing her heart until she reaches that last breath.

"What's more interesting," I continue, this time crawling over to her head. "Is what goes on in this mind, any mind at all. To get inside someone's head, you need to do more than what your body shows. You need to take a peek."

The knife, oh right. I reach between her legs and remove it, taking a moment to inspect the bodily fluids sticking to the blade. The blood is thick, almost black.

Blood pools, and I must move quickly, not wanting any of the pages to be ruined.

Checking her pulse, she doesn't have long now. Up to me, now, to expose what's inside. "The brother should have gone beyond the superficial torture. He should have understood the intimacy of an internal organ, being able to hold it, and best of all, understand its importance."

When she's no longer breathing, I begin making my edits. The blade works well against her pale skin. Once that's removed, I can pay better attention to what lies in wait.

An odor casts itself across the apartment.

"These are details that could really add to the power of your story."

One minor slip and it's the contents of her stomach pouring out. A blend of acids and alcohol, a partially digested burger, it flows. I take a step back, keen to remain vigilant, not wanting to waste a good observation. Details, details, details...

"Every single organ, exposed."

Ever hold a heart in your hands? No more of the figurative, the impression, rather the actual heart, the very thing that retains life? No, few do. But in Boll's story, here's the heart. I hold it in my hands, the warmth and weight of it palpable, something unforgettable.

"You got to make sure that ends up in the story."

Don't lose those kinds of details.

The brother violated, the brother took and left trauma, but he never understood what it takes to go inside, really inside. When I get to the climax, the most important part of the story, I know it'll require more than this blade. Thankfully, she's done a little cooking. Saves time, seeing that she's got a bone saw. That'll come in handy.

"To get inside, you need to see, touch, feel, understand the mind itself."

First attempt at cutting, my grip slips, the saw partially slicing her scalp. I wash my hands and give it a second attempt; it's better than the first. It takes a lot of effort to get inside of a mind, but I'm not about to do her wrong. I get through, and seeing it, the brain exposed, it's a sight to behold. Seldom do you ever hear what it looks like, its hue, and the smell...

"The final act consists of a callback," I say, before making the first cut.

After skin and muscle, there is only organ and bone. Remove the extraneous and you're left with an entirely new sight, something previously unrecognizable.

The best parts of her novel will debut as a decimation of her dead body.

Every organ, and every vertical slice of her brain, will be found placed one on top of each other, each given a chapter. Each set of pages acts as a plate, an offering. Take your pick, she's an open book, ready for your understanding.

I can't help but grin when it's over. I think I did a good job as an editor and story doctor. Every indication of the superficial, her skin and her looks, gone; all that remains is what's inside.

I'm glad to have done right by her, and to have made Chelsea Boll a masterpiece.

People will clamor over my body of work for clues, for answers, for inspiration. They won't know what to think, and they won't be able to look away.

Chapter 7

Pendel has never been the patient type. None of the editors have circled back and submitted their offers. Hendrix better give him what he wants. This is no joking matter. When Pendel manufactures urgency, you need to comply. This is about money. This is about power. This is about how Pendel can't sit in his own skin. After a good 20 minutes of repeatedly refreshing his inbox, Pendel needs to direct his anxieties elsewhere. Elsewhere meaning, what else? Social media. His notifications are forever maxed out, a ceaseless red that has become almost too easy to ignore. He scrolls through the timeline, making note of the day's literary discourse.

Fiction writers are talking about word counts again, what constitutes a short novel from a regular-sized novel. The hot takes vary but the vitriol is, for Pendel, predictable and borderline sad. So many writers seeking some clarity getting caught up in the weeds, becoming part of a conversation that goes in circles with only a handful climbing out of it with a viral post. The academic writers are busily expressing their annoyance with an article about fomites and how they work. The article was published by a reputable publication, yet its contents are rife with misinformation. It has sparked another debate about the continual dissolution between fact and fiction, cited sources and fluff pieces.

He notes J.D. CHURCH trending. The algorithm spits out the most relevant posts. People are still sharing their adoration, their grief, for the newly deceased author. Good, he thinks. Things are still fresh, perfect timing on an incredibly lucrative deal. If you scroll down a little bit, the beginnings of what will be Church's dark side are coming up for discussion and debate. The allegations won't go away, especially because, well, Professor Church made more than a few mistakes, hurt a lot of people, and let the power and prestige get to his head.

But Pendel doesn't scroll that far down. Instead, he keeps clicking around, hunting for something that might be spicy enough for a little schadenfreude. His favorite.

Where's the latest trainwreck?

A fairly well-known author is having a little bit of a meltdown, something about how they found out that they are blacklisted due to not selling enough books. Other authors chime in, expressing similar situations, how the whole industry is broken. One editor offers advice, definitely a bad move, because the author of the original post goes off, a caustic attack done up by a repost that looks like it'll go viral.

Pendel grins, seeing the irony of the entire act. Initially, it'll put the editor on blast. People will get so worked up that some will take sides and declare that they *will never let their agent submit* to the editor's employer, a mid-sized independent publisher in business for nearly 50 years. They aren't a new publisher on the block. Some people will go so far as to reach out to authors who worked with the editor. Yet as the anger begins to subside, as soon as a few hours after the initial virility of the attack, the author of the original post will be the one who looks worse. Editors watching in silence on the sidelines will take notes. Don't want to work with that author. Steer clear. Same goes for Pendel. Once upon a time, if he found out that the author didn't have representation, he would have offered to sign them. Now?

"Hell no," he mutters, moving away from that mess.

Refresh inbox. No offers. Come on, Hendrix.

The other editors, whatever; this isn't really about them. Alfred A. Wolf has an opportunity to single-handedly ride the J.D.

Church wave. Talking millions of books, millions of dollars. Just give Pendel what he wants. Meet his demands.

Checking his DMs, it's pretty much what he expects. Authors try to ask if he's open for queries. Authors trying to cozy up with Pendel, some trying the whole *saw you post about tactic*, attempting to bridge a gap, a boundary that Pendel has always built up. So what if he replied to their post, maybe offered a comment? These are authors of varying desperation. Sprinkled through are media requests, some bots, the usual. At least one attempt by a publisher, typically an indie, reaching out (why via DM though?) about potentially meeting, having lunch. One of those typical publisher-agent industry meet-and-greets, hoping to get on Pendel's submission list. Editors seeking the upper crust. Editors and authors trying to survive. Of course, they're going to try to reach where Pendel stands, a top agent looking down at the competition.

He's about to mass delete all the DMs when he sees one that catches his eye.

"That didn't go well, did it?"

What didn't go well? Reading it again, Pendel's mind can't help but string together two disparate topics. Church's passing, Detective Monroe. He checks the user profile, but it's an obviously fake name, "Deadly Reads," profile picture and the entire grid of posts consisting of book photos glamorously strung together with different slightly on-topic accessories. Your typical social media influencer fare. The account has under 200 followers.

Still, he just can't not say anything, and bothering to reply will be yet another poor decision, something Pendel will regret.

"Who is this?"

The original DM disappears, which disturbs Pendel, causing him to search around the platform, looking into privacy settings, and then finally doing a Google search, which yields the truth. The account has chosen to engage in vanishing mode. The DMs, once seen, disappear. The information sets him off, "I demand to know who this is."

"Just another author bemoaning the loss of a great one, while also disappointed in the publishing industry's treatment of such a grave loss."

Pendel falls right into the trap, "Yeah well this is an industry, a business, and it's about making money. Authors can value the craft all they want, but we need something that can sell. Church sells, and even better, he sells well in death too."

DMs disappearing...

"Tell me who this is."

He receives a thinking emoji, chin tilted upwards, eyes squinting. He's being doubted, and that's one of Pendel's triggers—being judged as something less.

"Tell me who this is so I can ensure that I never respond to your query!"

The author starts typing and then stops. A pause, and then, the message in full: "It sucks being stood up. Trusting someone and then having it end in rejection. Sucks that it happens all the time to authors. How often have you been stood up, rejected?"

Pendel snaps, "That's it, I'm reporting this account."

The DM disappears, leaving him with no evidence for Benji, no further steps to take. Pendel is stuck, blinded by his rage.

It's all part of the vanishing act. Pendel is in the mist, lost and being led by his emotions. This won't end well, and worst of all, this is only the beginning.

"I'll give you 60 seconds," Pendel says. "59, 58, 57..." With every subsequent DM, the paper trail fades.

Chapter 8

I'm often surprised at how easy it is to get under someone's skin. Pendel finally answers my DM. Took him long enough. Yet it doesn't take any more than a single DM to tap into the inner hostility, the demon within.

"25, 24, 23..."

He's counting down, demanding my identity. But what's the fun in that? I'm looking to drag this out, pull every nail from its bed, one by one. Like any good story, you must take special care in setting up the big reveal, the double cross, the truth that becomes fully realized after a series of deceptive acts.

Pendel makes for a great character. He assumes he's the center of every story, the protagonist, the very thing that breathes life into any story. Everyone learns the hard way...

How about a bit of a rude awakening?

"Did you like the pages?"

He stops counting down and I watch as the text bubble flickers. The guy must be surging with anxiety and anger. I can almost feel it from here, this coffee shop just down the street from Cooper Willis Endeavor's office. I like to be near, in some way, you know?

Sometimes it can be tricky, especially when I'm busy working, but I find that inspiration really comes to me when I can almost see it happening all around me.

His reply is terse, the guy is just not getting it, "I demand to know who this is."

"Ah, you didn't read them."

It's just too easy.

"Last chance, or I'm going to report you."

"Would you like me to resubmit?"

"Okay, that's it. You're going to be reported."

"That's A-okay with me," I say.

Everything vanishes, leaving him with this odd interaction, a glimpse of things to come. We'll talk more, and he'll turn to the social media platform. I'll get an email, but nothing will happen. If Deadly Reads dies, I've got plenty of alt-accounts.

Like the detective said...

"We'll be in touch."

Oh! How nice. My second acceptance. *Denver Review* wants to publish my story, "Insides." Think of the story like I think of Chelsea, my own muse, a perfect a memory to hold close. I had to write about it. The toxic sibling rivalry, the abuse, and the biggest reveal of all: what both characters carry within them. The editors loved the story. At a breezy 2500 words, I don't dawdle on much. It's intense, because to make a statement, you kind of have to, you know?

But yeah, this is great news.

The body of work adds up and only helps with the eventual deal(s) to follow.

Gives me even more motivation to keep moving forward. Who will it be? Really, I already know. A glimpse at Pendel's deal report, and if it isn't Church, it's got to be the author next up, Brendon Kawada. Lucky me. Looks like Brendon Kawada is *very* online.

I'm going to be his biggest fan.

His latest post, "The secret to being productive is being too poor to do anything else," and you just know I have to comment on it. Different account, Deadly Reads, you did well enough. I'll be Courtney Haim. They got an AI app for everything, be it a profile picture or header, it's all a click away, and there is no reason to waste any time; I let the AI fill in the blanks so I can step forward, a single comment, modest, "So true. I live paycheck to paycheck. There's no such thing as a day off." Kawada sympathizes with a quick and highly informal, "Truth, I feel you."

I'm already in. Jaw clenched, it's a tense back and forth, being careful yet clear enough that I'm yet another author, one who admires him. There'll be a DM, one where I discuss how excited I am to read *Mechanical Animals*.

"I just can't wait!"

Kawada is new, a debut author, so the flattery works wonders. It sinks right in. Frankly, I'm surprised at how easy it is for Kawada to open up. It goes from congratulations to talking about how I'm an emerging author. Giving a link to the story in the *London Review* helps. Mentioning that the *Denver Review* just accepted my story creates a noticeable pang of jealousy.

"Lucky you," Kawada says. "I've been rejected 4x."

"It only takes one!" I keep it cordial, establishing that we are peers, colleagues, authors facing the void. In truth, that will be my steady and methodical entrance into his story.

First, leave him hanging. Last DM being his, asking if I have an agent.

Leave it like that, no reply can get Kawada's mind racing. Maybe it's a sensitive subject. Something he shouldn't have asked. Now he may have someone who had been a fan turned into an enemy. It's a self-imposed spiral, a mind-fuck of micro proportions. And I'll leave it at that. My alt-account has 32 followers. I'm a nobody. He moves on.

Second, wait until the end of the day to reply back. Pick back up like nothing happened. Kawada will be so relieved that there wasn't any disdain that he'll reply back on impulse. Keep it brief: "Nope, no agent," and he'll reply with, "Oh you will." He adds, "Keep racking up those bylines and you will."

That's how it works.

The industry trades on the prestige, the merit of the byline. When it comes time, merit is tested, and the test... book sales.

Third, make him feel seen yet vulnerable. "You worried about the book selling?"

It can go either way, cold shoulder or a kind retort, but there won't be any room in between. He'll get back to me quickly, "Duh. It's a lot of pressure."

It is a lot of pressure, being judged by your latest book. That axiom has always and continues even more so every day to be the slogan scrawled above the gates of hell, the publishing industry declaring: You are only as good as your last book.

"It's good to be aware of what's expected of you," I say. "But all you can do is your best."

"Your best isn't always good enough," Kawada says. A warning for both me and him, yet I can tell it's more for himself.

"That's why it helps to be around other authors, part of the community," I say, leading into what will become the moment we meet under the awning of a bar on Park Ave. "There's a badass reading tonight. I'm going. You should go. Get out of your head a little."

He'll consider it, unwilling to confirm until the last minute.

I'll be there, standing with a vape pen, flavored smoke plumes, one after the other, counting how many inhales before he arrives, and I take his breath away.

Chapter 9

Pendel reports Deadly Reads under the pretense of harassment. He should feel better, the account will likely be subjected to removal, but it lingers, this feeling of helplessness. It's what he's felt every single time Alexander Moyer emailed, yet it could be his stubbornness that keeps him from connecting the dots. Then he gets a call from Becky on his personal cell rather than the agency line, "Oh, what now?" and it's all he can think about.

Stress level high, Pendel lets it go to voicemail, knowing that Becky will leave a message, offering an indication of the nature of her call.

"Henry? Henry. When you get this call me back. This is **urgent**." End of message. He waits a few minutes before returning the call. It's evident that she's upset. The magnitude of the current moment—her husband's dead, everywhere she looks there are reminders of her loss—he expects her to be wafting between the stages of grief. With no one else to turn to when it comes to the business side of things, Pendel's at the top of her contacts list.

Maybe she even thought of them as friends. Pendel never saw it that way; though it'll later come out that he exhibited preferential treatment, carte blanche, to J.D. Church and looked the other way when Church abused his power. All because Pendel was too busy nursing his own fixation on prestige, nursing the latest pour of bourbon, the latest sales figures, and just how unstoppable both he and Church seemed to be.

My author. For Pendel, it was always about the money.

Inbox, nothing. No new offers. He checks the time. It's still early; they have a bit more time. Pendel still can't shake the feeling that he'll hit a few speed bumps.

For now, fine, he'll pretend to care.

"Becky, you called?"

She's been crying, he can hear it in her voice, out of breath, "I don't know where to start."

"You're going through a lot," he says. "We're going through a lot. I have to say, though, we're on the verge of getting an offer! Jerry's work and your livelihood are all taken care of. Which reminds me, did you look into his files, on his computer, cloud drive, all of it? What are we working with in terms of unpublished work? Knowing how productive he was, I'm hoping that there's dozens of novels we can work with. I can only imagine how many years of exciting new work his readers will be able to enjoy."

He expects Becky to join him in celebrating, quick to lighten up and offer him the good news: tons of manuscripts discovered, a veritable long list of novels, memoirs, short stories, and more. J.D. Church had always indicated to Pendel that he was working on multiple projects. It was kind of expected after a few years of representation.

Becky's silent, and then she breaks down, sobbing as she accuses him of being insensitive, "How can you think about making deals at a time like this?!"

Pendel shifts instantly into damage control: "I understand, really I do. This is tough, talking about business when he's left us so recently, but you need to know that I'm doing this in honor of Jerry. All the books he's published, and everything he wasn't able to give his readers, this is my duty, as his agent, *and as his friend*, to usher into motion."

"No!" Becky interrupts, "You're not telling me the full truth."

He doesn't follow, "I have no reason to withhold any information."

"Yeah? Is that so? Then what about a certain Detective Monroe? Hmm? Did he not pay you a visit?"

How did she know? Fact: The detective has already made his rounds. Tread carefully, he tells himself. "He did," he says. "He had a few questions for me. Mostly getting a handle on our professional relationship."

"And he didn't ask you anything about Jerry's tenure at the University of Georgia?"

"No," he says.

"I don't believe you, Henry," she says. "I know he asked you about what happened, and the fact that you didn't just come out and tell me is really hurtful. I should have heard it from you, not from some fan showing up at my doorstep!"

"Wait, what?" His heart starts racing, mouth dry, nerves tensed. "I don't understand."

"You understand completely," says Becky. "It takes a fan at my doorstep and then a detective calling me up, sniffing around about my husband, thinking that maybe the murder was vengeance, and then you're not even remotely interested, or even showing any signs of grief, talking instead about how much money you're going to make."

She's talking too fast for him to keep up, "Becky, please. What's this about vengeance?"

"...and this fan, can you believe it? This fan shows up and has a tattered copy of *Harvest Falls* with her. She takes it, starts tearing pages from its spine, one by one, and then sets them on fire. I'm already exhausted, and then I have to put out the pages before they ignite the dead leaves or something. This fan, they tell me that Jerry got what he deserved. They tell me that they think it is vengeance, that it's karma for all that he did to her. Do you know what he did to her, Henry? Because when she signed up for his workshop, I don't think she was signing up for that."

Pendel's mind goes back to the allegations.

Shit. He didn't think it would come up so soon.

"He told me that it wasn't true," he says, instantly regretting the disclosure. In the context of this conversation, it confirms what Becky suspects.

Pendel has been withholding the truth; he had known about the allegations when Becky clearly hadn't. A fresh new laceration, Becky can only react in anger, "He wasn't a person to you, just a payday. He was also a monster."

"He's more than a payday..."

"I think I need to seek legal counsel."

"I have a lawyer," he says.

"I need one that isn't on your payroll. I need one that isn't in bed with you and your reputation."

"Becky, you're upset. Please—"

She hung up on him.

The entire conversation came out of the blue, completely unexpected. Now what? Pendel sits in silence, in complete shock. Without any means of processing the events, Pendel returns to his default, the inbox open, no new offers. He becomes suddenly determined to jolt one out of an editor, to get things moving.

Chapter 10

Take his breath away. Kawada certainly needs it. Needs to get out. All that sitting behind a screen, fixated on social media discourse, has his mind all warped. It makes telling his story that much easier. If I'm honest, I see him walking up to the bar and I sideline him at the street corner, preferring to jump ahead. No need for exposition. The plot is simple. Kawada's young and impressionable, the world equally an exciting and scary place. His dreams are nothing short of any author's dreams: accolades, bestseller status, a long career full of wins. Yet I'm here to help him make sense of what pockmarks any career: the losses.

For every loss, there's another layer of defense, thicker skin, but he doesn't know that yet. I'll have to show him the layers, peeling each back until he's fully bare.

"Hey, Brendon, right?" I can tell that he's surprised, but also the moment he sees me, he cools off. I'm exactly the opposite of what he expected. Personable, charming, playing into his preferences. His story is perfectly exposed: lonely, young, not yet fully aware of his feelings, much less his own self. His identity is a blur of expectations. He went to school for creative writing and always wanted to be an author, but never questioned why. The romantic notion of creating worlds with a single thought, spinning together sentences that open doors from which readers step into and are forever changed.

Or really, it's because Brendon's most comfortable in his mind, escaping into his imagination. He has so many fantasies, it's enough for a dozen novels.

For tonight's workshop, we'll explore one of his favorite fantasies.

"Hi, Brendon." The way he smiles tells me that we can move right along. Not like he wanted to sit in the audience listening to people read in their poetry voice for an hour.

Leave it to me. I'll set up the premise.

I gesture to the front door, "It's whack. Like three people in there."

He's nervous, so I tell him it's okay. "We haven't walked in, it's not like anybody's going to notice."

Nobody's going to notice. So we take a walk into the night, the start of his fantasy. At first there's not a lot of banter, mostly just me talking about my own writing. Better to be honest, the subconscious can tell. "Rejected," I say. "Haven't found an agent yet. But hey, I'm feeling better about things because I've been getting a few short stories published."

"Right, right, you told me! I'm so jealous. The *London Review*!"

He remembers. Good.

"Right! Thanks. Though I'm the one who's jealous. You got signed to the best agent in the business, the jackal himself, Henry Pendel, and your book was sold to FSG, one of the top major publishers in the world."

But he can't enjoy the success because he is worried about their expectations.

"Whose expectations?"

"FSG, Henry, everyone," he says. "I feel like I just got lucky."

"Ah yes, imposter syndrome," I say, giggling.

"Ah so you're a member of the club too?" He laughs. A sign that he's comfortable enough to head over to the park, the one I picked precisely for our discussion. We keep with the industry talk until we make it into the park. That's when he starts to get some déjà vu. I'm the one talking up a storm, going on about my novel, *Friends Selling Friends*.

"It sounds fascinating," he says, but I can tell that it's bothering him.

When we sit next to each other on a park bench, he begins to catch on, "Wait a minute..."

"Looks familiar, doesn't it?" I say, gesturing to the darkened park. "Same location as where your two main characters get rid of the bodies."

"How is that possible?" He doesn't know how to hide his fear, hands woven together into mock prayer. "It was fiction."

"Brendon," I laugh. "Come on now, just because it's fiction doesn't mean that it can't come true. Isn't it a spitting image?" I bet he wants to know how I've been able to read his novel. I'll save him the trouble, "Oh and I'm a reader. I'm such a voracious reader, I don't like to wait. When I hear of a book that's enticing, I find a way. I found a way." I move closer, our legs touching, "I always find a way."

Now that he's primed, we get to the story and its faults.

"You're nervous about disappointing people, well I'm here to help!"

My toolset, the trusty tried and true, it starts with the blade, the most intimate of utensils. "Your novel is equal parts romance and horror, with gothic undertones. It reminds me of that bestseller from way back. The one with all the shades of grey."

When I show him the blade, he starts begging for his life.

"Brendon, hush," I say, pressing the blade against his leg, "I'm offering my feedback."

And he even apologizes, "Sorry..."

"It's okay," I say, unbuckling his belt. "Like in that book, yours is a little too fixated on the vampire as a vampire, when really, isn't a vampire someone that cannot escape their own demons? They are forced to live in an in-between state, unable to enjoy a moment because it has already passed. They cannot be intimate because everyone they may connect with will die. Well, unless they're another vampire, which in that case, there's the part about incompatibility. You get that right, insomuch as it's new and original, the two vampires literally draining each other when in each other's presence."

His pants pulled down to his knees, I take the blade and begin to cut little perforations on his inner thigh. The blood drips off to the side, and he starts to get an erection.

I point it out, "See? My feedback will make for a better story. Your novel could do better if you really focused on that draining." When he's fully erect, I take the knife and cut horizontally across his stomach, deep enough to drench his shirt and lap. His boxers stick to his penis, and to illustrate my point, I take the knife and direct it to the shaft. "When you're dealing with vampires, you really got to focus on the blood. In all respects, the blood, drainage, life itself, the source of what makes us unique." And cut, the blade goes through clean, and then it's a little geyser, all that blood that had collected in the muscle, engorged, now a nice showing for the workshop. A little show and tell never hurt.

Dear Brendon passes out from the pain. A group walks by the park. They see us both on the park bench, and I lean in close enough that I feel his warm breath against my lips. Just to make it look like we're making out until they pass by.

"That's a shame," I say, when they're gone.

Kawada wasn't paying attention. His story could have used another revision.

Chapter 11

Fact: Becky is disgusted by Pendel's behavior and actions. He doesn't care what she thinks. That's none of his concern. She can see him as what many have said, "a jackal," but he's never cared much about the impressions of others. They all better stay away, respect him, and play nice. They don't want him to get mad. Jerry's widower better stay in her lane.

He calls Benji and tells him to be on the lookout, "Seems things are picking up since Jerry's passing."

"I see," says Benji. "I'm looking into it right now."

"Good, because I don't have it in me to even bother doing a search."

He can hear Benji's keyboard, fingers tapping in a flurry of keys. His lawyer will discover the current situation, which has spread quickly, beginning with a social media post that was picked up by TMZ and other media venues. "This is public record," says Benji. "It's only a matter of time before the two instances of assault charges are discovered."

"He has a record?"

Pendel never bothered to look. Church's publisher and management must have paid a company to bury all the information.

"He does," says Benji.

"Then how did his wife not even know?"

"Hmm, it seems your client has been quite adept at covert operations, if you catch my drift."

"No, I don't. Spell it out."

"He has two misdemeanor charges and one felony. Like I said, it's public record. The reason nobody bothered to look is because he made a good show of being a public figure, active with constant in-person events and interviews, always active on social media."

"He was good at social media," Pendel says, a gut response. "He's tried to teach me some things, but I just couldn't get used to documenting my life."

"Yeah well, it worked for him, clearly."

"It did."

While he's on the phone with his lawyer, he gets an email from Emily Mills at FSG. Pendel's heart skips a beat; now's the best part. He only really feels alive when he's chasing down the best offer, negotiations are so much like a sport. Who gets the upper hand? Who picks apart the other person's defense, finding a way to weed out another counteroffer?

"Hey, got something. I'll call you back. Important business."

"Yeah sure," says Benji.

Pendel can't wait to see the number, his hand shaking as he guides the cursor to the bolded email. Upon opening, he is greeted with the first of many passes. Mills keeps it brief, clearly not wanting to burn any bridges:

Mr. Pendel,

We at FSG have been at this for a few hours now. This has become an urgent and halting decision to make, one that we do not take lightly. In fact, this has been the toughest call of my career thus far, and many of my highly experienced colleagues have said the same. We're big fans of the works J.D. Church has given the literary world, but considering the allegations and reports coming out, we do not feel it is morally right to publish an offender. Again, this is a tough call. I hope we can work together in the future; you have quite a talented list of authors!

Pendel is insulted. It's basically a form-letter rejection. In his eyes, at least, this is about as by the books he's received in years. Do they forget who they're doing business with? This Mills has no idea. Pendel's livid, believing that her inexperience has just destroyed her career, and marks a visible point where her luck has run out.

"If she thinks she's getting any of my help now," he laughs. "Oh, I can't wait to see when she realizes just how big of a mess she's created."

He takes the pass personally, knowing well that he shouldn't, and in the heat of the moment, he calls Hendrix. It rings but the editor doesn't pick up, which only adds to Pendel's frustration.

"Marina!"

There's nobody else to turn to.

She appears at the door, "Yes?"

He falters. Nothing comes to mind. "Umm."

How uncharacteristic. Pendel's always been vigilant, determined to get the best out of every situation and conversation.

"Are you okay?" she asks. Bet she has heard by now.

"I am always okay," says Pendel.

She frowns, "It's just that first Church is found dead, they say murdered, and then it comes out that he's sexually abused his students... this is a lot to handle. For anyone, but even more so for your because—"

"Because what?"

The guilty always act defensively.

"Because he was your author."

"Right," he nods, tension instantly deflating. "Right..."

Marina's just trying to help. It's her job.

"Need me to call up... maybe Benji?"

"Already did," he says.

"Oh, okay."

"Yeah."

"Yeah."

She's just standing there...

"Well okay then!" Pendel claps his hands together.

Marina can't help but ask once more, "Are you sure you're okay?"

"Didn't you hear what I said? I'm always okay."

The hostility is enough to get her to leave.

Pendel already knows: There's going to be another pass. He's trying to come to grips with the situation. Did Church ever tell him about his criminal past? Had he and Pendel simply ignored the confession? Money speaks louder than honesty.

"Hmm," he mumbles.

And... there it is. The next pass is from that guy at Macmillan. Pendel rolls his eyes, "Of course. He'll go along with any hot take." He clicks, opening the email. "Fucking coward has no spine. He goes for the easy offers, the low-risk projects."

The pass goes something like this:

Henry, Thank you for blah blah blah in light of the recent news we blah blah blah I've always been a fan of blah blah blah...

Pendel doesn't even bother to read the whole thing. He files it away under Church and skims the other new email waiting for him. Sandwiched between queries is a media request from a journalist. He doesn't need to open the email; they want a quote. Everyone's going to want a quote from him. *My author...*

My agent.

The synchronicity, everything is colliding at once, and he isn't liking any of it. Pendel's seeing everything fall apart. And then Pendel finds himself back on social media, reading people's takes on Church, when a DM appears from a new account, the name and profile picture look obviously fake.

"Ever wonder what people are saying about you behind your back?"

The message sent harkens back to a voice that has been whispering in his ear, watching his every move, since the beginning of the story.

Chapter 12

Do you ever wonder what people are saying about you behind your back? Does someone like Henry Richmond Pendel feel anything? Does he even care about backchannel gossip, people sharing their experiences with the agent? He'd like the public to believe that no, he doesn't care. He doesn't even listen; this is all business. When really, I know he looks. I know he has his assistant looking. I know what eats away at his sanity, hyper-analyzing the day when everything changes, and he no longer is a top agent.

He can't help himself.

I know this to be fact. It's proven yet again when he replies to my DM.

That's their business, not yours. Not mine. Who the fuck is this?

Vanish. It all vanishes.

Well, except for the bodies. Like any good story, it sticks around. It stands the test of time. People remember, and they return to an emotionally impactful story.

Another acceptance! This time it's with the *New Yorker*. That's right, the *New* fucking *Yorker*! Seems Brendon Kawada had been tapping into the zeitgeist. Everyone's feeling lonely and abandoned these days. I blame it on technology. It was designed to bring people together when really all it does is tear people apart.

Everyone is seemingly there, at your fingertips, when really, you're in a cage, watching the infinite scroll of discourse and outrage. Kawada poured his heart out, just as I ensured that the outpour from his heart wasn't wasted. I had a taste. There's nothing more intimate than someone connecting with your story. Second is swapping body fluids.

He didn't get mine, but I surely got a taste of his.

I could still taste it, the life coursing through that thick blood. I got a taste just before it finally left him. And then I returned to his manuscript and made the changes accordingly. I found the chapter that stood out and stood alone. He could say so much more, but I find it to be the most tender and heartfelt of the entire manuscript.

Still, he could have really run with it, have both characters on the edge of the would-be cliff, willing to hurt themselves if it meant other people would no longer hurt themselves.

Isn't that beautiful?

You can find beauty anywhere.

So my story, *Cliffside at the End of the World*, is going to grace the pages of the *New Yorker*. How fun!

The *London Review*.

The *Denver Review*.

And now... The *New Yorker*.

I hope the third time's a charm!

Hey. Respond.

Oh, he's making demands! To be at the receiving end of Pendel's cutthroat commands...

Hello.

He's ready to pounce, *Who is this?*

I'm ready to play.

He's typing, continues to type. The text bubble flickers but there's no reply, not at first. It gives me time to draft a future email to the agent. He'll get it when the timing's right.

When his reply does arrive, it's lengthy, roughly upwards of 500 words.

> Look, I am not a person you can toy with or threaten. You do realize who you're talking to, right? This false sense of security, this anonymity of being on the internet, it isn't going to keep me from finding out who you are, and when I do, you better believe there will be repercussions. I have pursued legal action before, and I will do so again if you do not stop harassing me with these messages. Now, if you comply with my demands, telling me who you are, what your name is, and why you see this as an adequate avenue of communication, I may waive any future legal repercussions.

There's more but it's repetition, the extraneous stuff in a story that's unnecessary. Take in point the brevity of my reply:

Those are serious threats. I'm an author, hopeful to have an excellent career. I'm also a fan of yours. Your list is full of amazing authors. I hope to one day be among them.

To the point. Best of all, it's all true.

I am among them.

He gives me another rambling response, mostly about how I refuse to provide a name, and it's precisely the reason why this is a malicious attack, one that he won't just shrug off. *And if you think I'll be offering representation, you must be out of your fucking mind." He then adds, in a successive reply, "Yes, you are absolutely out of your mind. I think I'll be blocking you now.*

Blocking the account works similarly to these DMs, they disappear, become invalid. What no longer exists can't be used as evidence. Or didn't Benji tell you that's how this worked.

He doesn't reply. Now I really have his attention. The key to plotting is to prolong the big moments, giving them just enough buildup to have the biggest impact when it's finally time for the hefty scene. Case in point, here's where he gets another clue:

I've been workshopping my stories. With some of your clients actually.

Now why would I say something like that? I wouldn't dare put myself in a compromising position if I didn't already know how this story is going to end.

Still nothing from Pendel. He's being good for once; perhaps there's recognition of how much is left in this story. He must see it now, that we're only getting started.

The thing about people talking about you behind your back is that you don't have any control over it. It can be so frustrating for someone in your position, especially when it involves these murders. I say murders because there's been more than one.

He starts typing, but it's better if I give him a nugget of truth, this time before the public finds out.

When was the last time you spoke with Brendon Kawada? Because I had a productive workshop the other night, and boy, he's talented. He really bleeds onto the page.

Pendel won't be saying anything else. He realizes who's in control and where this story is going. The emerging author has a lot to prove.

Chapter 13

People refer to him as a jackal, a hungry and unrelenting presence in the literary world. Pendel finds himself doom-scrolling using search terms exclusive to his name, reputation, and agency. What he finds is more negative than positive, the latter being almost entirely on an author's part, the many deal announcements he brokered, the many opportunities he fought for and was able to make a reality... but nobody talks about how much skill and determination is required to get an author the deal they deserve. No. Instead, there's nothing about Pendel except the many authors rejected, often by letter or silence, who turn to their blogs, their social media accounts, and to their own writer communities to talk ill of him.

He does get a kick out of those actively frightened of him, an indication that at least one major aspect of his cutthroat business dealings has yielded something intentional and deliberate. They wouldn't dare cross him, and that sense of fear, Pendel doesn't seem to fully understand, is tantamount to the same "power" mobsters and other criminals use to scare their victims into silence. Pendel has a lot of work to do before he can even see past the immediate issue, his current flood of anger and anxiety, before he can fathom how the reputation he has built may very well be the thing that destroys him.

And then there's the call. Hendrix, who else?

Watch an entire empire crumble.

Pendel picks up by the third ring, never a good sign when it's a call directed to his personal cell phone, yet Pendel must uphold that reputation. He can't demonstrate any hesitation. No matter how anxious, he must remain steadfast and stoic.

"Hendrix, been anticipating your call!"

He doesn't get the same enthusiastic response. Instead, Hendrix remains calm and cordial, "Pendel, how are you faring?"

"Doing just fine," he says.

Maybe that's not the right response, given the admittedly grave circumstances.

"I see," says Hendrix.

"Out with it," Pendel says. "You've got something for me. I know you do. Ticking clock!"

"Right," he sighs. "Well, I'm sure you've seen the news stories, and the furor online."

"Yes, so?"

"Henry, really? That's not for nothing. Did you know he had a criminal record?"

Pendel nervously clicks around his desktop, cycling through different browser tabs, until he falls back on his social media account. There, waiting for him, is yet another DM.

It's in his past, Hendrix. Jerry is rehabilitated.

The DM: *Kill your idols.*

That feeling again... it's more than a feeling of being watched. It's a feeling of being... known.

Hendrix isn't so quick to discount all the allegations, "I thought I knew the guy, and maybe I did. It's tough, attempting to hold onto the good times, and all the great books he's written, after hearing about that pattern that sounds like a textbook sexual predator."

"Shouldn't we all believe that a person is capable of change?"

"I'm not in the mood," the editor says. "I'm here to deliver the bad news."

"Seems we've already heard the 'bad news.'"

"Well, there's more," Hendrix says.

Another DM: *J.D. Church's stock plummets. Publication date: Postponed.*

It's Moyer.

"You didn't call me to give me bad news, did you? After all we've been through, and after all that I've done for your career... Hendrix, you didn't just call me to give me bad news? Imagine the repercussions..."

There's nothing a person can do, not even someone so conditioned to feel and think of nothing except for the next benchmark of success. This is going to be a pass.

"The publisher won't allow it," says Hendrix.

"Sharpe?! Oh, let me give him a call..."

"No! No, this was my decision," Hendrix says. "I'm not putting in an offer. In fact, in light of what's come up, I don't think it's the best time to invest so much in the J.D. Church estate. Perhaps three books a year for a decade... that might be enough shelf space for someone. Maybe it's time for Church to be laid to rest, given a long breather."

Pendel can feel his heart race, the vitriol surging through his body. Through grit teeth, he says, "If you pass now, you pass on Church forever. Think carefully Hendrix. I'm giving you one last chance."

"It's going to be a pass from me, Pendel," he says. There's no changing his mind.

"If it's a pass on Church, it's a pass on my entire client list," Pendel warns. Maybe it's not the best idea, putting his entire list in jeopardy. Alfred A. Wolf is one of the biggest and most venerable imprints in the entire trade publishing industry. Losing that lead will cause a significant decrease in earning potential.

The threat does receive some hesitation from Hendrix, but inevitably the editor defaults with, "It's unfortunate that we couldn't see eye to eye. I've always enjoyed working together."

Losing his cool, Pendel shouts, "Of course you enjoyed it: I made your career!"

Hendrix retreats, saying his goodbyes, "Sorry I'm not calling with better news. My condolences, Henry. These last few, I don't know how many days, have been insane."

The call ends.

Pendel attempts to call back, but his attempts go unanswered.

Another DM, *Invest in an emerging author.*

It's Moyer.

The Church estate, an untold amount of monetary potential, hangs in the balance. Pendel must find a home for the work. If he doesn't, it will be more than a mere financial blow to both him and Jerry's estate; it'll tarnish his reputation in a manner that will follow him for years. Every deal is weighed on by the agent's previous dealings. Henry Richmond Pendel couldn't sell J.D fucking Church?! Nope. Can't happen.

It's up to that editor, the one at that indie. He traces back his email threads, finds her name, Rebecca Morrison at Concept Press. It's time to make that call.

"Hello, this is Rebecca?"

"Rebecca! This is Henry Pendel."

There it is again, the hesitation, her response being opposite of his expectations. "Hi there, Henry."

"Hello! I'm calling to check in on that offer. Ticking clock! We're getting down to the final few; I'll be closing soon."

"Ah, yeah." Here it comes... "Pendel, it's quite the opportunity, really. When you contacted me, the inner Church fan in me screamed loudly. I couldn't believe it."

"Great!"

"But then I started to believe it, seeing why a work of Church's would make it into possible acquisitions here at Concept, I see it now. I was suspicious. Here at Concept, we're as venerable as the Bigs, but we also understand that certain authors of a commercial magnitude are unattainable and unmanageable for an indie press. Church should be one of them. Then the marketing department saw the article in TMZ and then the one in *The New York Times*, and it all started to make sense. Henry, you can try all you want to persuade me but the answer's the same: We're passing. There's too much baggage on this one. It sucks because I am such a fan. I'll always enjoy what Church gave us, but on a purely business decision, there's no way we can be host to this controversy, much less invest as much money as it would require to be the host. Thanks again, Henry, really. I hope you have a better day soon. Oh, and my condolences."

That's it. Call ended.

She hung up on him!

Pendel sits at his desk, completely stunned. What to do now?

How can things get any worse?

A notification.

It's Alexander Moyer.

His entire body shakes as he opens yet another DM, *You should hear it first. It seems your author, Brendon Kawada, has passed away. How unfortunate. It seems he really took to heart my advice. He really bled on the page. Let it all out. A sacrifice for the sake of the story.*

Another phone call. Pendel picks up but can't speak.

It's Benji, his lawyer.

"Pendel, it's not looking good."

What does Moyer know?

Chapter 14

I really should celebrate, but I've been holding out until the right moment. When I match with her, I figure the moment is now. There's a Thai place near the park called Slowloris. Make sure to get there after her, so that when I approach the table, there's a modicum of edge, a first impression as dramatic as it is memorable.

"Wow, you're more beautiful than I imagined," I say, giving her hand a kiss.

She stands up, shy and slightly blushing, "Hi, you look great too."

We take our seats. Some small talk.

"Alex, is it?"

"That's me," I grin. "And yours is... Marina?"

She blushes, "Yes. Marina Grace."

"Wow, sounds like a great name for a character in a book."

She rolls her eyes, "Oh, well thank you. I know that's supposed to be a compliment, but I'm surrounded by all things books and publishing all hours of the workweek." She frowns and offers a confession, "I kind of hate it."

"Hate... books?"

She nods slowly, "Pretty bad, huh?"

I laugh, "At least you feel something about them. Feel like most people see them as decorations for their latest IKEA furniture purchase."

She laughs, and right then and there, I recognize that I'm in. The bond begins.

I check the phone, DMing when the timing's right, but otherwise my undivided attention is hers. I've studied the dating scene, read countless academic articles about the dynamics of human bonding, yet it pales in comparison to, you know, actually going on a date.

Shouldn't I be nervous?

The answer is no. This is an interlude to a song, a preamble to something precious. A story needs its own vulnerabilities, its own blemishes. It needs to fail first to succeed.

Instinctively, I reach for one of the menus folded shut on the table even though I already know what I'm going to get. Just like I know how every part of this will play out. It's been practiced. I practice *everything*. Nothing in life worth the effort must be relegated to first drafts.

"Well, it's very nice to meet someone as honest as you."

"Oh come on," she says. "I'm kind of surprised actually, both of us matching. I've never had much luck with the dating apps. I always hear from people that they can match with dozens in minutes but," she stops and sighs, "I don't know if I should tell you this but, whatever, you're the first person I've matched with."

"Wow, really," I say, eyes fixed to the pictures on the menu. "Well, same for me too. You're the first I've matched with."

"Really? Somehow, I don't believe that," she says.

I look up from the menu, "I guess you'll just have to trust me. I believe you."

"I guess I will have to believe you too," she says.

"So, I guess this is where we ask about each other's lives, day jobs, that kind of thing," I say. "You start, since you've basically already started. What do you do?"

Marina sighs, "Fine. I guess I'm a secretary and an assistant."

"You guess?"

"Yeah, because I kind of do everything. I read submissions, I send rejections and acceptances, I look through contracts, I deal with author issues... I make coffee, I clean the office, I attend agency-wide meetings, I even handle bills, groceries, and basic adulting."

"Wow," I say. "I hope you're paid well."

A comment made intentionally to provoke, which works swimmingly. The years of being abused by Pendel have festered and begun to cultivate in this woman. This anger, it creeps in for only a second, long enough for her to offer an illuminating rant:

"The whole industry is shit! I'm being paid $39k. That's after taxes! Only reason I'm still working this gig is because I haven't found a job that can pay the same or better. My life is basically working tirelessly for a stuck-up agent that can barely function without me, and go home, scavenge for food, call home asking for more money, and continue to apply for jobs." She stops, exhales, and asks me, "How many jobs have you applied for?"

The server interrupts, "What would you like?"

"Uhh yeah, I'll have the bibimbap," she says.

I'm grinning ear to ear, ordering the Pad Thai and a round of drinks for us both. Besides, it's a celebration; it's the beginning of a great night. I'm learning so much.

"450," I say, after the server leaves.

"What?"

"You asked me how many jobs I've applied for. I like the number 450."

She shakes her head, "Almost, 388. It's absurd. How anyone can live in this city..."

"Eh, I wouldn't call this living," I say, a partial joke. "Most are here to indulge in fantasy."

She leans in close, "What's your fantasy?" Her attempt at flattery.

"You're asking me what I do?"

She winks, waiting for my reply.

"I'm... an emerging author," I say.

More difficult than expected, saying it with a straight face.

"Have you been published?" There's that industry side of her kicking in.

"Yeah, a few," I tell her, casually name-dropping my bylines.

She's impressed, "Really?"

I wink, "You could say I have some experience."

"*London Review* and the *New Yorker*, those are heavy hitters."

I'm an emerging author, hopeful yet ignorant of the inner machinations of the trade publishing industry. Play that angle up perfectly, and she'll be a valuable resource.

"Are you writing longer fiction?" she asks.

"Funny you should ask," I say. "I'm working on a novel."

She doesn't yet know; the Alex sitting across from her is the same Alex who had been rejected, likely by her own hand. Where there's Alexander Moyer, there's also Alex P., "new transplant looking to make a real connection."

Drinks arrive and we toast, "To good things!"

She offers some advice, "An author needs to go out there and be really competitive."

"I agree," I say, making a move. My hand gently placed on hers, she doesn't recoil. In fact, she slowly but surely reciprocates, our hands held there, draped across the table.

"So, what are you afraid of?"

She thinks about it and then says, "Being a failure. You?"

"I'm an author," I say. "I get that fear of failure. Hmm." I pretend to struggle over my inevitable response. "Maybe not being able to look back and see what I've accomplished."

At the end of the day the only thing that spoils is your own ability to appreciate what you have achieved.

"I get that," she says, clearly finding me endearing. "But that can't stop you from continuing to write."

I shrug, "We all have a story to tell. Some are just willing to do anything to tell it."

Part Three
REPRESENTATION

Chapter 1

Debut author **Chelsea Boll**'s **INSIDE**, pitched as *Night of the Living Dead* meets *The 40-Year-Old Virgin*, is about a forty-something mailperson living a boring life when she meets a man who's eerily similar to her in every way, she starts dating him only to see her friends back away one by one, suspecting that it might be him, and not them, to **Hailey Slaughter** at **Tempest**, in a major deal, by **Henry Richmond Pendel** at **Cooper Willis Endeavor** (NA).

How did it happen? That'll be the first thing Pendel will ask when he sees the deal announcement, same question the detectives will ask when they see her body carved into parts. That's all part of the reveal, I should know. I've planned it out, the moment of rejection became a moment of pure, unadulterated vengeance. Got to hand it to Detective Monroe; he saw right through my MO, down to the pathology of victim and villain. It *is* vengeance, and it's one of the purest forms of concentrated obsession outside of a need to possess another.

The deal announcement is nestled unsuspectingly in Monday's marketplace update. I get a notification, and it's bittersweet because you see, Chelsea Boll should have been alive to celebrate the confirmation of her first book deal, her words finally set to be printed onto paper, bound together for an experience offered to the unsuspecting reader.

And after our workshop, it takes an entirely different meaning. Much more profound when you see the deal announcement paired with the discovery of the author's body.

The timing is frankly perfect.

Her body in pieces, her body more than the sum of each individual part, they'll find her long after each organ has begun to wither, no longer fresh. She manifested it as truth...

I remember.

She didn't feel like she was a priority to her agent, and she certainly didn't feel like she was a real author. Sometimes life imitates art. Chelsea, dear Chelsea, her body and life ended, yet it took people over a week to notice.

Work left a few messages. Some acquaintances texted her, at least one grew frustrated because she didn't respond and proceeded to send a flurry of messages before going silent. No calls. No knocks on the door. Nothing. It was the landlord who found her pieces; it's in the lease, the right to entry when it's maintenance or an emergency. In this case, the next-door neighbor reported some pests. You see, they were saying that there was some kind of smell, almost indescribable, but the sudden appearance of roaches elevated the urgency of bringing in an exterminator before things grew to the point of infestation.

They knocked. After receiving no response, they even came back at the end of the day, another series of knocks, and again, nothing. The landlord made the choice, giving them the go-ahead, and then it happened instantly, the powerful aroma hitting them. So intense, it knocks the wind out of a person. They pause, they do what they need to do to recover, but they're going in. Curiosity has been piqued. What are they going to find?

The culmination of our workshop. Case in point—the heart cradled by a chapter, a stack of pages that have since begun to curl at the edges, a mock embrace around the organ as it has begun its descent into decomposition. I would have liked for them to be able to read those pages, but they took their sweet time. And it'll take some time for them to figure out who it is. Chelsea Boll's name is on the lease, but identifying the body cannot be left to assumptions.

Detective Monroe. What do you think?

Quite the mess, huh? Just look at what happened with the brain. The source of the pending infestation, but it's not what the exterminator had expected. The roaches scatter, but there's something burrowed into the brain matter. This part nobody can plan. The best you can do is hope that it plays out right. Burrowed deep in her brain, a sizable rat has taken the opportunity to feast. A week's worth of neglect has attracted a scattering of vermin. This bold rat is caught off-guard when the exterminator reaches down with a gloved hand. It screeches and runs away, its escape plan already figured out. Everyone recoils in disgust. Quite an image.

This all happens late in the afternoon, sunset well on its way. They're too busy reacting to notice a bystander, yours truly, cross-legged and watching from the safety of the fire escape. I have a good sense for these things. Spent a lot of time waiting and then it became clear, Chelsea was correct. She was underappreciated, rendered invisible because she didn't have the cache of an author cut from the Ivy Leagues, the cutthroat literary communities. Poor Chelsea, she loved writing, but how could she handle the hurdles of becoming an emerging author?

When Monroe shows up on the scene, I'm already descending the fire escape. His presence implies the merging of both plot lines.

I'm feeling good, tired but good. It's been a lot of shadow work, hiding and being invisible. The fun part is being able to workshop the story, continue building what will surely become an impressive body of work. I keep reminding myself of the end goal, how this all will end.

What about Pendel? Is it all coming apart yet?

He knows it's me. Pendel must be the first to know, or else the story doesn't add up. First suspicion and fear, then knowledge and anger... finally, when I once again make my presence known, it won't be like at Black Swan, brunch and confusion; he'll look into my eyes, feel my presence, and understand the weight of what's in store. For me and for him.

After knowledge and fear?

Next comes complicity and self-destruction.

The world around him will fold over and take on an entirely new, more menacing shape. He'll be forced to let it all go if he's going to make it to the end of the story. If he wants to stand toe-to-toe with me, he's got to lose it all.

I'm doing my part to make sure that happens.

He'll thank me later. This story's going to be one for the ages, studied by authors and agents, critics and readers.

Chapter 2

Pendel learns about the Boll announcement from a horror newsletter, one that he isn't even sure he signed up for. Chelsea Boll is one of his authors. If he were honest with himself, he would recognize that he lost track of the author amid his perpetual hustle to glean the best deals for his top clients. This Chelsea Boll does have a file folder at the agency, and if he were to look, he would discover a signed agency contract and author questionnaire. The latest addition would be a contract, also signed, by what looks to be his signature and that of editor Hailey Slaughter at Tempest. It's all there, facts waiting to be found. Yet Pendel sees the deal announcement, feels an overwhelming sense of confusion, and immediately receives a phone call, one that draws his attention away toward the latest issue.

It's all been emotional whiplash. First the failure to sell J.D. Church's estate, not to mention the postponement of the recently announced *The Renegades*. Then the allegations and information of Church's predatory past going viral. Then he hears from Benji that his widow is going to press charges against Pendel and Cooper Willis Endeavor. What's at stake? All previously published and brokered works.

Never mind the looming presence of someone or something that has been at the center of the conflict, who eludes Pendel's ability to fathom it. He already knows it's Alexander Moyer, he simply refuses to give it any attention. He cannot accept it as true, much less face the apprehension and fear that has begun to mount.

He should be mourning the loss of his authors. After Boll, that makes... three?

Oh right, Pendel has already forgotten that fragment of information. It's a future problem. For now, Pendel doomscrolls. He refuses to acknowledge that he has a meeting with the detective, precipitated by the fact that the very same author he has "supposedly" just aided in finalizing a book deal has been found brutally murdered in her studio apartment. He refuses to think about how this looks for him, the agent with three dead authors and counting, the agent being paired with J.D. Church in the posthumous criminal past controversy; he refuses to look at what people are saying in the media and online about Chelsea Boll's death, just like he paid little attention to Brendon Kawada's tragic death.

His doomscroll is pointed and exact, focused only on one topic: The war overseas. He fixates on every story, real and fabricated. He ignores emails and phone calls.

Pendel doesn't pick up for Benji, who has only one thing to tell him: *I think it's best if you pursue different legal representation.* The lawyer has an entirely well-thought-out explanation that goes into plenty of detail. In reality, his long-time attorney is not cut out for the sort of work that's increasingly likely to follow. An entertainment lawyer specializing in copyright law, Benji is intimidated and unqualified for what Pendel will require. Yet Pendel won't take his calls, won't answer his emails. Text messages? Consider them dead on arrival.

Everything shuts down, an internal and external quiet settles in, a calm before the storm.

Marina checks in, poking her head into his office, "Do you need anything?"

No answer.

She understands.

When the lone meeting scheduled for today draws near, Pendel closes all browser tabs, takes his cell phone, and places it face down on the desk. He sits in silence. Maybe he should be preparing for the meeting. It could be worth getting his story straight. But what does an agent do when the situation at hand involves three dead authors?

Nothing to do but wait.

Pendel stares blankly at his inbox, eyes unfocused, everything blurring together into a mess of confusion and color.

"Mr. Pendel."

The voice of interrogation. Detective Monroe stands before him, arm outstretched.

Blinking, vision clearing, Pendel takes his hand and says, "H-hi, hey there." His voice cracks, saliva and phlegm scraping against his larynx. He clears his throat and tries again, "Hey there. Sorry about that." He takes a sip from his mug of lukewarm coffee, "Where did the day go? I guess I've been drowning in it today."

"Life of the agent, I assume," says the detective. He crosses his legs, reaches into a pocket, and retrieves a device. "Thank you, again, for taking the time."

"Of course," he says. "This is quite a trying time; I don't yet believe it's hit me as reality."

The detective doesn't waste any time. "I have a few questions," he says. "Where were you the night of Thursday, June 7th, at approximately," he checks his notes app. "At approximately 2:41 AM?"

On the spot, Pendel is in no way prepared. "Umm, asleep, I'd imagine. Asleep at home."

The detective narrows his gaze and then types something into his phone. "When was your last communication with Brendon Kawada?"

Kawada? Why him? Pendel isn't following, yet offers the best answer he can give, "Oh I'll have to look at my email to confirm, but it must have been recently. We just signed the deal with FSG!"

"Hmm, and Chelsea Boll?"

"Chelsea Boll... who?"

"Your client?"

Pendel shrugs, "Doesn't ring a bell."

"You just announced a book deal this morning? That Chelsea Boll."

His piss poor memory always backfiring on him. "Ah! Sorry, my mind is always so scattered. Right, yeah." He's got nothing. "Again, I'll have to check my files but hey, I like to be prepared before a meeting; I wasn't aware we'd be touring my client list. I thought this was about Church."

Detective Monroe maintains his poker face, letting Pendel talk himself into a corner.

"After recent events and breaking news, I have prepared as accurate a—"

Monroe interrupts, "Those allegations are very disappointing. I was a big fan. There's a lot of noise surrounding the case. I'm here to talk about the death of Jerimiah Church, Brendon Kawada, and..." he checks his notes. "Chelsea Boll. Your clients."

It's not like last time.

Pendel has become a person of interest. After so many years of being the one with the power and ability to intimidate, Pendel feels the shift, suddenly he's on the defense, the foundation he built breaking apart as he struggles to keep it together.

"Okay, understood. Well, I'm an open book."

Monroe crosses his arms, "Last time we spoke, you discussed the importance of maintaining a professional and equal relationship with your clients."

Pendel nods, "I did, yes. It's important."

"Okay, well, how do you account for the text messages we've found in this," he reveals another phone, "Church's cell phone."

Pendel's flustered, "I don't know. I was drunk. I, umm..."

"I'll read them for you," says the detective. He takes a moment to retrieve the text thread. "There's a whole back and forth here, late at night, lots of discussion about book deals and death. Some banter about an author's legacy... and, here we go." Detective Monroe pauses and then reads with a slight inflection in his voice, "'I'll leave behind enough projects to ensure a healthy posthumous career.' To which you reply, 'That's why you're my favorite client!'"

Monroe looks up from the phone, gazing intimidatingly into Pendel's eyes.

Pendel does his best to maintain a sense of calm. In his left hand, he texts Marina, "Come in here now. I need out of this stupid interrogation." She replies, "What do I say?" He texts a quick, "Anything. Lie!"

Pendel sighs, "Wow, I have no recollection of that exchange."

"Is that so," the detective says. "Do you feel like your drinking has gotten out of control recently?"

Marina walks into the office, "Mr. Pendel! Hey, sorry. Umm, something's come up."

"What is it? I'm in the middle of something," Pendel says, gesturing to the detective.

"It's Becky, she's on the phone."

There's his out, a near escape.

"Oh my, I see," he says, doing his best to act sympathetic. "Well, umm..." Putting the detective on the spot: "Were we almost done here or?"

Detective Monroe isn't easily duped. He's seen this movie before. Shallow decoy to delay a guilty suspect's inevitable destruction. Alright, the detective plays along. The delay will give him enough time to piece more of it together. Besides, Monroe isn't the one that'll continue to unravel, defeated slowly yet surely by a vicious onslaught of guilt and anxiety.

Detective Monroe grins, "Nothing we can't pick up at a later date."

Pendel gets a stay of execution.

Chapter 3

Ride the height of a brand-new day. I enjoy a leisurely stroll through the suburbs of Long Island. The safety net of a home and a local community is what so many people here are buying into, and I kind of love it, the idea of settling down, no longer in the hustle of being seen; rather, you've felt the highs and lows of a career, and it's now about building a sanctuary for when the traumas of your younger years, your ambitious years, flare up and what you need most is a hug from a loved one, an honest moment disengaged from the furor of the outside world.

I'm a tourist, tapping into this energy.

"Morning," I say, offering a little wave.

She doesn't recognize me, and why should she?

The dog runs across the front yard, up to the sidewalk to sniff me. His snout presses against my black boots, the once-over continuing up my legs when finally, the dog seems to get a scent and his tail begins to wag. I pet the top of his head lightly, a little rub behind the ears.

"What's his name?"

The owner walks up to me, "She. Her name is Pearl."

"Aww," I grin, lowering to a crouch. "She's adorable. You're adorable, aren't you? Such a good dog. A good dog."

My attention may appear to be on the dog but really, I've been down this block over a dozen times. The other night I sat in a car rental, watching from the other side of the street as she, acclaimed author Mallory McAllister, and her husband ate dinner, followed by their usual falling asleep in front of the TV. The simple routines become the most comforting.

My attention has been on every detail. My approach has everything to do with the author standing before me. McAllister has published a dozen books and has written twice that number. Though she had early success, her career has been in decline, every new book receiving a smaller advance before eventually her last novel, *The Haunting at Dusk,* was sold to a new indie press for just under $2k. McAllister has always been a writer's writer, each novel being completely different from the one before. With such range, McAllister has developed a cult following. Yet she doesn't do many readings or literary events. In the last three years, she moved to Long Island to focus entirely on her two kids and her craft. It helps to have a partner with a successful meat packing business to help build that safe place. McAllister just finished her latest book, *Half,* and it's different. Give it up to the time and space, or perhaps her finally accepting what she cannot control, particularly the various moving parts of the publishing industry, the preference for sales and accolades, and her long-kept bitterness carried along through the years. The noise gets pushed aside and, in its place, she has finally started to understand what keeps her motivated and inspired.

"Hi there," I say, turning my attention to McAllister. She looks exhausted. "Beautiful weather we're having, huh?"

She yawns, "Hi, yeah. It's great."

"Works well for the mind, all this sunshine," I say. Pearl whines, demanding more pets. "Hey, she really likes me."

McAllister's turn for chit-chat, "Out for a stroll, huh?"

I nod, "That's what I'm doing!"

She chuckles, "I always plan on a walk, but I can never wake up in time."

"Not a morning person," I say.

"How can you tell?" She lets out another yawn.

"Well, I'm not much of a night person," I say.

"Yeah, well," she trails off.

We both look down at the dog, my hand still petting her soft fur.

"You live around here?"

Right on time, I smile, knowing where this will take us. First steps, the baby steps, I'll tell her that I live in the next neighborhood over, one called Glenfalls, which I have also traversed, plotting out how the next chapter of the story unfolds. I'll tell her the superficial details of what it looks like to come off as a kindhearted neighbor: architect, commutes into the city (yeah, it's exhausting), long-term partner but not married, thinking about getting a dog (attention once again given to Pearl), no kids, but my partner has been thinking about it, could stand to lose a few pounds (the comment receives a genuine laugh).

When it comes down to a name, I don't need to hide, not this far into the story.

"Alex," I say. "Alex Moyer."

"Nice to meet you, Alex." She matches the cadence of my introduction: "Mal. Mal McAllister."

She's shortened her name, a soft dodge of sorts, because an author two decades into her career, she's beginning to undersell her craft, choosing instead to be simply Mal, a person. A neighbor. But I'm here specifically to draw out an author.

"Mal..." Play out a slow realization, putting the names together, and then, "Mallory McAllister?" Pause, for impact, note her slight discomfort. "Like the author. Mallory McAllister. You're not the same, are you? Wait..." Then I'm narrowing my gaze, because McAllister has plenty of author photos, pictures of her on panels and in interviews. "You're... no way."

She takes a step back, her body tensing up, "Yeah, the same."

"What are the chances... *My Time in the Heartland* is one of my all-time favorites!"

Normally an author loves attention. Normally meeting a fan of their work is tantamount to seeing their work come alive. It's worth all the effort it takes to complete the story.

McAllister isn't one of those authors. She freezes up, almost physically uncomfortable while I chatter on about my favorite parts of the book, how it changed my life. None of that is true, mind you, but boy do I enjoy seeing her squirm.

Who did this to you, made you this way? An author fearing attention, shying away from their fans, is an author traumatized by the machinations of an industry designed to capitalize on their work.

"You know I'm a bit of an author myself," I say.

That gets her attention.

"Yeah? That's great," she says. "Come on, Pearl."

"Oh, but Pearl isn't done getting her pets," I say, grinning.

"Pearl," she whistles. "Side!"

She raises her hand, the command to join her, yet Pearl remains at my feet, my hand stroking the back of her ear.

"The dog's on my side, not yours, Mallory."

"Wait, what?"

It's right around here that the author begins to understand that I'm writing myself into her story. This encounter was deliberate, right down to our subsequent discussion over some tea. "What have you been working on since you ran away and hid from an entire literary community?" She still has her hand raised, palm out, when I approach, grabbing her with some force. "Actually, let's go inside. We don't want to talk about such a sensitive topic where others may hear, you know?"

The dog comes along, and we step inside the hermetic author's abode, a lived-in safe space that will soon be the site of my next workshop.

Today, I get to see it for myself.

Chapter 4

Marina wasn't lying. That widow *is* on the line. Pendel just can't get a break. He sees the detective out and brings in yet another pain in his ass, a potential sore point for his reputation and forthcoming career. Marina looks concerned, "Do you need me to tell her you'll call back or...?"

He shakes his head, "I got it." A deep exhale, this has all been so exhausting. "Thank you, Marina."

Before leaving, she turns to ask him, "When was the last time you left the office?"

He blinks, no answer to give. Time has run together. The office itself has become his cage, or maybe the truth is he cannot stand the thought of venturing into public, not with what's happened.

"You have to take care of yourself," Marina says.

"Thank you," he says, when really his tone registers as *you may now leave.*

"Yeah," she says. Marina cares far more than her pay grade. She'll return with clothes, shirts still in their store packaging, folded pairs of pants clipped and pristine; she will bring him take-out, ensuring that he eats. The care is undeserved. Pendel didn't ask, and if he could see this from the outside looking in, he would agree: Someone like him doesn't deserve such care and compassion. Everything that's happening is a consequence of his actions. It was only a matter of time.

When he's once again alone in his office, he picks up the phone, returning to that trained voice, ready to receive Becky's anger.

"Hello Becky," he says. "How are you faring?"

Much to his surprise, she doesn't come out spitting hate. "I can't believe it. I really can't. They have taken his name and turned him into a costume, a thing people can put on and brandish as an example of cruelty." She sobs, "When really, they are the ones being cruel! He was a loving father, and I know he loved me. What he did... I still can't believe it, but that's not him. That's not the Jerry I know and loved. He must have lost himself to his demons, his writer's ego; they say he did all these horrible things to women, his students, yet what about the punishment he has already endured for crimes he's committed? Jerry wrote from a place of darkness, and the same people who loved his words now condemn him."

Pendel agrees, "They should be remembering him for the work he gave us, not the dark past that he has already atoned for."

It's something he said. Becky raises her voice, "Oh, don't you fucking start!"

"Hey now..."

"I'm not calling for your sympathies! I'm calling because I'm legally obligated to do so in accordance with the lawsuit I am filing against you."

"Lawsuit..." Pendel starts laughing. "You can't be serious, really?"

He isn't laughing at her, rather at the circumstances. What else can go wrong? Well, how about this: "Oh, you think this is funny?"

There isn't enough time to explain himself, "No, I wasn't—"

"Yeah, well let's see if you think it's funny when the same people condemning my husband realize that his agent motivated him to be the disgusting person he became."

"How are you going to prove it?" There's the Pendel everyone knows and fears. The moment she tries to threaten him, Pendel lashes out, becoming the same vicious negotiator that an entire industry has become receipt to and unpleasantly familiar with. "In fact, what you're saying is so far out of reach, I'm frankly surprised any lawyer would believe that you have a case."

"Oh, don't you worry. Dear me, you will regret that laughter."

"I find that hard to believe." Pendel believes there can be no case. It's the work of a shady lawyer, someone who sees the dollar signs and will surely bleed the widower dry. Maybe the lawyer sees an opportunity, all the media attention only benefits him as the lawyer representing the plaintiff in a case as tragic as it is disgusting. Well, for the defendant, anyway. Pendel is on the losing end, no matter what happens. He'll lose money; he's already lost money. He'll have his name and reputation smeared... though again, that too is inching closer to a reality. And then there's the matter of his own personal worth, which was always based on the magnitude of deals he amassed. He keeps his mind set on the fallout of J.D. Church, the loss of that lucrative book deal, and how poor it'll look on his agenting abilities when it gets out that nobody, not even the small presses, dare put in an offer for exclusivity to the entire J.D. Church unpublished estate.

"You're a monster, you know that?" Becky can't stay angry. She's too much of a wreck to meet Pendel with the same unyielding determination. "You don't care at all about your authors. You use them and abuse them and manipulate them for the sake of your own enjoyment. I'd say you were in need of help, but a person needs to recognize that need before anything can be done."

The call ends. Pendel believes he came out on top. She has no basis for such an outlandish claim. That widower is processing her grief and lashing out at the people who have her and her late husband in their best interest. If anything, she should be asking Pendel for help. What needs to be done to ensure that Jerry's name is unscathed?

Somewhere deep in that inbox of his, there are emails sent and received between Pendel and Church, where they chat about book-business related items, yet peppered throughout, some exchanges have images attached. In some, there's a rating system, out of five,

five being a *stone cold hottie I'd like to fuck* or a SCHILF. The rating is supplanted with a review from both he and Church, followed by the steadily increasing implication that the young women in these pictures aren't being rated merely for their attractiveness; they're being scouted, Pendel encouraging Church's fragile ego to pursue his students. In numerous instances, Pendel lives vicariously through Church's mayhem, and there are some emails where Church isn't sure if he should, yet Pendel pressures him to go through with it or else he is a *loser* or a *coward.*

The most damning line in their correspondence: *If I were you, I'd do them all. No one would even say no. They all want to be with a genius.*

Pendel never finds the emails because something demands his full attention. Another email, the first in what feels like weeks, from one Alexander Moyer. Subject line: **Workshopping.** Pendel's heart beating in his chest, the feeling's the same. It was him. It was him all along. Everything falls into place.

Dear Mr. Pendel,

By now, you should have figured it all out. It's a shame you didn't join me for the last workshops... but good news is I'm about to begin my latest workshop! You should join me.

An address, additional details, and best of all, an attachment, a picture of what looks to be a mouth taped shut. The title of the jpeg, "MalsManuscript."

Mal.

Pendel looks at the image and then the email a second time and then it clicks. The email, it says it all. He's got him! The proof he needs, right there in plain language.

Pendel whispers, "Got you now, motherfucker."

Chapter 5

Of course, he'll think he has the upper hand. My email being the slipup that begins my inevitable capture. Yet he doesn't yet know what's at stake. He doesn't know who he's about to see again, after all this time.

Give him a few minutes to feel like he's going to be okay. Better than okay. Give him 10 minutes, and he'll think he's a hero. Reputation fully restored. But I won't give him 15, because then he might think he's still got a chance.

No. I've had enough time in the shadows. The moment has come, the part of the story where the two protagonists meet.

It won't be a follow-up email. Rather, he'll get a text message. So unexpected, the number quite familiar. Who else? Why of course, it's Mallory!

He remembers Mallory, right?

Guess who, I say.

Takes a little bit to draw out a response, but it arrives, oh it will arrive. It'll be as plain and derivative as his DMs, *Who is this?*

Duh, I say. *Are you saying you deleted her number?*

It would be understandable. Though she is technically one of his clients, one of his authors, Pendel and McAllister have silently distanced themselves in the last few years. In line with her departure from the city for Long Island, McAllister carries a knot of hurt and betrayal that could have only come from someone close.

Pendel should have apologized, but he isn't the sort of person who can see both sides of a tragic encounter. All that history, McAllister's career made and potentially broken by Pendel, and yet it truly comes apart with a miscommunication, Pendel lacking finesse when telling McAllister that her work no longer has the capacity to sell.

I'm blocking you, whoever this is. MOYER.

He's getting defensive, but I've got the perfect retort. *Oh, I wouldn't if I were you. You know Mallory, she's got a lot to say about you.*

That'll get him, and any attempt at gleaning any additional information will just leave him spiraling. An offering to join the workshop, this time with directions.

Better get going, I tell him. *We'll be starting the workshop soon.*

Pendel has a drive from midtown Manhattan through to Long Island.

Author Mallory McAllister's house is in every way a perfect setting for a workshop. It is pristine, a sanctuary built around family and solace. From the walls adorned with pictures and paintings, to the fact that every square inch of space in the house has been defined by its members, to the lived-in look and odors, this is the McAllister home, and I can do nothing less than compliment her on such a great home.

"Really, it's something. This is a home away from all that hurt," I say. "You've done well."

Pearl follows me into the kitchen, where I proceed to lay out everything I may need for the upcoming workshop.

"Home alone? Everyone else at work or school?"

She follows me into the kitchen, her attention instantly on the knife, the same blade that has made so many edits. "Yeah..."

"That's nice. Everyone staying busy. Gives you some peace and quiet to write during the day, huh?"

Approaching the kitchen counter, she reaches for the knife.

"It's okay, you can hold it," I say. "We both need to feel comfortable if we're going to have a productive workshop."

I refill the dog's food dish, the hefty bag of kibble hoisted over my left forearm as the circular kernels clatter into the metal dish. The dog looks at me and wags her tail before proceeding to devour the food.

McAllister holds the knife, testing the sharpness of the blade with her index finger.

"I take my craft seriously," I say.

She nods, "I can tell."

You've got to appreciate an author who is willing to take a risk; go with him rather than make a whole fuss about how they factor into the story. McAllister's experienced; she has written about a wide range of topics, everything from coming-of-age to the human condition. What use is fear if it prevents you from a full understanding of what's at stake?

I sit down at the head of the dinner table.

McAllister sets the knife down and joins me.

I lean forward, feeling even more excited than initially expected, "So, what are you working on?"

She sits there, shoulders slumped, "Nothing." She lets out a deep sigh, "What's the point?"

"The point is creating a body of work," I say. "The point is creativity, everything that makes it onto the page. The point is leaving a lasting mark, one that forces people to look at what you've created, demanding not only a reading but also some understanding."

She remains downcast and lifeless, her voice stuck in a distinct monotone, "That's your opinion. No two authors are alike."

McAllister has let her failures win, leaving her talent as a storyteller to atrophy in a self-appointed prison sentence. Her reputation in the industry may be marred due to low sales, and her own impression of her author career tarnished to the point of having become traumatic, yet it was McAllister who chose to leave the ranks of authors, stepping aside from the ever-bustling concourse of literary events and conferences to become miserable in this house.

"You had a bad run of books," I say. "It shouldn't prevent you from attempting to write a better book. That's the beauty of a story: Where one ends, there exists an opening for another to begin. You have fans. They've been waiting for years. They want a new story from you."

That gets her attention, "Huh, I can't stand social media, the internet, whatever. It gives me severe anxiety."

"You got fans. They have been waiting for a new book."

"Yeah, well, that new book didn't sell. Worse, I wrote another book, and my agent couldn't even bother to look at it. He's put me on a blacklist, signed but insignificant."

Here's my opportunity. Besides, for this story to be perfect, she's going to have to choose a side. One must become the villain, and the other must become the victim.

"Who's your agent?"

I can see how much she hates saying his name. And I'll mirror her distaste, saying something about how he's got a reputation for being mean and bullish, *always getting what he wants,* to which she'll agree, but offer yet another nugget of insight. He ranks his authors, offering preferential treatment to the ones that yield him the best sales.

If I were jaded, I'd be inclined to say that every agent ranks their authors, but I want dear Mallory on my side. I must look like yet another victim of Pendel's wrath. This must look like vengeance, a shared opportunity for her and me to **get him back**.

I text him, *ETA?*

Text bubble, followed by nothing. He's so flustered he can't even type correctly.

15 minutes.

"Great!" I wave the phone in the air, "Our guest will be here soon!"

Chapter 6

Pendel instructs the driver to let him out a block and a half from the route's destination. Leaving the driver a big tip ensures that they will be less likely to remember driving Pendel to the proposed location. He's nervous, and there are plenty of reasons to feel this way. His legs feel heavy, each step dragging and prolonged; labored breaths lead to further panic as he reaches the house. He recognizes the vehicle parked in the driveway.

Turn around and leave.

Maybe it's not too late.

Mal...

No, the story is already in progress.

Pendel walks up the front steps. At the door he takes a moment, just one second, to stop and feel, no distractions or text messages or multiple threads of thought all to do with deal negotiations, who wronged who, and what is next on the to-do list. He just... feels. Feels a deep burrowing sadness, not unlike what he felt when his sister died nearly a decade ago. And it's too much, too tender and vulnerable to take on, so he pushes it back down, the feeling that this is the last time he'll recognize himself, and he knocks on the door.

Moyer answers the door. He excitedly reaches for his arm and pulls him inside: "Pendel, come, come, inside! We're ready to get started!"

He joins Mallory at the kitchen table.

Moyer waves the knife in the air, "Today's workshop, you see, we couldn't proceed without you." He inspects the edge of the blade. "You see, Mal's story here, it's incomplete."

Pendel doesn't say a word. For once, he understands where the story is going.

"Mal has had quite a career," he says, sitting down at the head of the table. Hands folded, he dons the role of a figurative professor, "Ahem, but a career is more than bylines and publications, am I right?" When Pendel doesn't say anything, Moyer chuckles, "You think I can't pry the story out of you? It reads better if you speak freely." Moyer looks around the table, "We're all here of our own free will!"

Pendel doesn't say a word. It's how there are no restraints and nobody is bound against their free will, which proves to Pendel that maybe he wants this to happen. After so many years of dodging and defense, being a workaholic and egomaniac, what he wanted most was to be punished.

"Mal was talented," Moyer continues. "She was... past tense. I speak in the past because you see, something was indeed taken from her. She had a few wins and many losses, but she was acclaimed. Her peers enjoyed her writing and best of all, she was a literary citizen. A damn good one. She ran multiple reading series in the city, offered workshops, and even helped teach emerging authors from inner city high schools. Mal did it all, and she did it for the right reason: She wanted to help. Yet how this story goes, shifting from present to past, it had everything to do with mismanagement."

Pendel exhales deeply, "Yes I know."

"Of course, you know!" Moyer laughs, "But you didn't want to tell it, and now, it's too late. It's too late for this story, but hey, there are still a few chapters left. Maybe you'll get to make a few edits?" Moyer thinks about this and then drives the blade into the wooden table. When he lets go of the sheath, it stands tall on its own. "To continue, the topic is mismanagement. Mal here, she had the best agent in the business. Maybe he still is; that's all up in the air, right Pendel?"

Again, Moyer attempts to get a rise out of Pendel.

Pendel remains silent.

Moyer grins, "This agent, he had ranked her in his personal little hierarchy of favored clients as in his top three. He would answer her text, email, call, anything in moments, no matter the time of day or night. It got to a point where she began to rely on his wisdom, and then his attention, before finally no longer being able to function as an author without Pendel's daily texts and calls. We all know this story, don't we?"

The room is silent.

Pearl whimpers.

"Need more food? Maybe some water?" Moyer dares him to fetch some more kibble, maybe a treat. "Be quick about it, Pendel."

This could be his moment. The part of the story where Pendel attempts an attack, or texts someone, anyone, maybe he dials 911. Instead, the moment of courage passes so quickly. The dog is given more food, some water, and a rawhide, which she enjoys, jumping up and down as he pulls it from its wrapper and hands it to the dog. She runs into the next room; Pendel sits back down at the table.

"Mal became codependent," Moyer says, now in a near whisper. "She was manipulated to the point that when this agent landed a hot shot author, none other than J.D. Church, suddenly Mal became lost in the shuffle. Imagine the emotional whiplash of going from having a person you trusted with both your most personal thoughts and your career to… them ghosting your every message."

Moyer points at the knife.

Mallory leaves her seat. Reaching for the blade, she stops and looks to Moyer for approval. He nods once, giving her the go-ahead.

"She finished a book," Moyer continues his tale. "It could have been great, and it was in many ways her best. It felt like a breakthrough."

Mallory approaches her agent, knife held tight in both of her hands. She lowers the blade, pointing it at his chest.

"The manuscript is the book her fans have been waiting for, a novel about half the world's population dropping dead, and how those, the HALF that remain, deal with a world cut down the middle. It had the makings of a harrowing tale of post-apocalyptic fiction, and she was so excited. Yet when she sent it to her agent, expecting his honest and kind feedback, what she got instead was a deafening blow."

She drives the blade into his chest, narrowly missing any major organs.

"It was a deafening blow to both her confidence and her creativity," says Moyer. "And then her agent proceeds to tell her that he cannot sell the book, or any of her books, that she is no longer saleable as an author."

The blade still lodged in his chest, Mallory's entire body begins to shake, reliving the traumatic events while Moyer tells it.

"And if that wasn't enough, the agent blacklists her, giving her busywork, telling her to write this book and that book, only to never do anything with the many finished manuscripts that dear Mal tirelessly wrote on deadline."

Pulling the blade from his chest, Pendel finally speaks, a nonsensical flurry of gasps and groans.

"Great of you to offer your opinion," Moyer chuckles. "But that won't be necessary. So many deadlines. As an author myself, I couldn't even imagine. It's why I've taken matters into my own hands." He points at her, "And taught her that the one thing she has control over is how the story is told."

Pendel presses his palm firmly against the wound, feeling the blood pour out warm before turning cold.

"How many deadlines were there, huh Mal?"

She takes the knife and goes in for another strike.

Moyer shouts, "No!"

She stops mid-strike, the tip of the blade mere inches from Pendel's neck.

"One stab is enough," Moyer says, standing up from his seat.

"No wonder." He walks over to her, "You do have that tendency to overwrite."

Moyer grabs the knife, wipes it clean on the sleeve of her shirt. He grabs her by the neck, Mallory choking against his grip, and shoves her back down in her seat. "Time out."

"Let me show you how I work," he says, turning his attention back to the wounded agent. "By the time we finish, you'll be such an important part of the story; it won't be complete without you at the center of it."

Chapter 7

Dear Mallory should get her moment of vengeance. From one author to another, I let her take my knife and give back a little bit of that pain. Just having a little fun, you know? Let the defeated author have her shot. It's good therapy, and it works double because it helps break Pendel down into pieces. Maybe it'll be enough for him to finally let his guard down.

But this is still my story to tell, not hers. She gets her little moment, and then I get things straight—her bound to the seat—and she doesn't even struggle.

Pendel won't be too difficult to keep, Mallory's stab wound rendering him defenseless. Yet he's all chatter, fighting through the pain like saying anything now will change anything.

"How's that? Tight enough?"

"Yeah," she says.

I'm frankly surprised at how willing she is, enough that I need to ask, "And you're okay? You're fine with this?"

"Yeah," she says.

"Oh you can give me more than that, Mal," I say.

She looks over at Pendel.

"Hush, we'll get to him," I say, clapping my hands together. "You liked how it felt, didn't you, getting a chance to hurt your agent? You like how easy it was to hurt him, that blade just so effortlessly cutting deep into his chest?"

She nods, "Yeah, I liked it."

"You liked it so much that you wanted to strike him a second time," I say, inching closer to the matter at hand. If the story is going to work, I need this author to play along. McAllister needs to sacrifice her life freely. "Am I right?"

"Yeah," she says, coming down from the adrenaline. Her eyelids are heavy, shoulders and arms hanging low. "You're right."

"Stay awake now," I say, giving her a slap. "The workshop's begun!"

Dear Mallory is restrained to the dining chair with zip ties, wrists clamped to the armrest, ankles bound together, more for her sake than mine. The body can withstand a lot of punishment, yet it often is its own worst enemy. Like the human mind, it winces and withers against the possibilities; every stab, cut, and suture causes physical trauma that can result in dear Mallory's body giving in sooner than expected, and we really don't want that.

The story needs to trim away all but the bold choices, Mal's final stance, and what will become this—an act of sabotage. Because that's what I'll need to ensure that Pendel doesn't get any ideas. He's full of it, untrustworthy, the gamut of all things that I despise. I've taken it personally for too long; now's the time to take it straight to the vein.

First prompt: "Mal, what part would you like to cut first?"

The way she examines her body, eying her chest, and then her arms, followed by her hair hanging over her face, she doesn't waste any time. "The face, start with the face. I would like to be unrecognizable."

"That's bold," I say. And once again, "Are you sure?"

She is.

"So be it."

A little incision starting from behind the ear, removing the cartilage and skin; there isn't a lot of blood, not at first. By the time I'm removing the other ear, the blood trail becomes visible. After the ears, next comes the nose.

Right before I aim for a swift removal, I ask her again, "Are you sure?"

"Yes."

"Are you ready?"

She nods.

This edit proves to be much more severe and debilitating than the previous, enough that she starts to cry and whimper.

"Doesn't matter how tough our skin is," I say. "Some edits *really* hurt."

Her face is a sheet of red. Already, McAllister is barely recognizable.

Second prompt: "Mal, what do you think is overwritten?"

It takes her a little to form her feedback, "I think… the fingers… toes."

So be it. This time, there are no warning shots, no pausing to see if she's primed for the next painful cut. I go for all ten fingers and thumbs, cutting one after the other in such swift succession that the nerve endings don't have enough time to register each removal. I'm two steps ahead by the time she starts passing out from the pain.

Another slap, and she's awake.

"Every cut and every slice, we do in the name of who?"

"My agent," she says.

"Your agent," I say, glaring at him, slumped over on the floor, voice already hoarse from all his begging, his confession muted, neither her nor I are willing enough to listen.

We got so much left to edit.

Third prompt: "Mal? Mal? Okay, if you had one last thing you'd change, what would it be? Take your time. You don't need to rush…" I notice the pool of blood at her feet. "Though maybe we should be a tad bit hasty."

Her reply will arrive. It will arrive and it'll come from the depths of the pain she's felt all these years. "I wish I never signed with…"

"Ah," I snap my fingers. Loud and clear. I'll translate that to Pendel; you get to watch me take yet another client of yours, another mark against your name. These are people, not products.

Authors are vulnerable to every single stage of the publishing process, and yet the one there designed to shield and deflect, aid and honor a safe and healthy professional relationship, failed this author. Dear Mallory, she is in such physical pain, but at least she no longer has to worry about dealing with the trauma.

Taking her feedback in stride, my editing involves the trimming of skin. It's easiest where the skin has some slack, soft and youthful. I'll do my best to trim her down until we see the person, the reality underneath.

Pendel has so much to say, but who is really listening?

Trimming skin from her face proves to be the toughest.

And then she's done, a body in half, brittle to the bone. There's still a pulse, just barely.

I lean in and whisper, "Thank you, Mal. We found your half."

She can now expire, give into the sweet relief of her final few breaths. She got what he deserves, and no that isn't a typo. Her body became the full exposé of what he inflicted upon her, and my, my, it's a horror story.

Mallory McAllister may not get any new book deals, but by way of collaborating with me, she got her chance to make a lasting impact.

This is the latest addition to my body of work. I'm finally seeing all my efforts pay off. And soon, I'll find representation.

Chapter 8

Pendel fights through the pain, yet there's not much he can do. His body fails to cooperate; lifting an arm means enduring a punishing wave of agony so intense that he loses all sense, vision blurring. The lone sense that never fails is the one that he would desire to be muted or made silent. He hears them, two separate voices, Moyer and... Mal. Of course, how could he forget? Why does he forget everyone? Pendel struggles with the pain like he struggles with understanding why he can be so neglectful. Yet there can be no revelation, only the pain of the stab wound dominates every thought. Attempting to stand up, his knees buckle, and he crashes to the hardwood floor shoulder-first. Every feeling amplified, inspiring him to give it one more chance. He makes another attempt to move, only to see that his body refuses any forward movement. There on the floor, he can just barely get onto his hands and knees before the wound once again calls to him, demanding that he coil his arms, pushing against the lifeblood pouring out from his chest. Defenseless, he concentrates on every breath.

Mal, what part would you like to cut first?

Hearing Moyer, he tenses up, and all that emotional weight unacknowledged suddenly releases, as though Moyer's own inquiry triggers his years of denial to finally, here and now, as he bleeds into his lap, to shatter and become a time for confession.

"I…" His voice cracks. "I am your agent, Mal. I was always your agent. My words spoke louder than any actions, and for that I'm sorry. Really, I'm so sorry, Mal. Please don't hurt her. Please! Don't, no!"

But it happens, ears and nose removed.

He sees her face, the dark hole where her nose had been, and he launches into a fit of anger: "You fucker! You're going down for this. I have those emails, and I have those messages. I've screen-capped them! I know your name and I have every single email dating all the way back to your original query. I have your response to my passing on representation, and I even have your socials, all your fake alt-accounts, recorded. My lawyer is building a case, collecting all the data, connecting the dots! You're done, you do know that? The end goal for you isn't some author career, it's a jail cell. It's having you incarcerated somewhere where the death penalty doesn't exist, so you get to waste away in prison for the rest of your life! You'll waste away, and I'll make sure that you won't get to write a single word. Even if you somehow pull some Marquis de Sade shit, writing on toilet paper or whatever, I'll make sure that nothing you ever put to the page will get out. No one will read a word. Your story will be forgotten! You are nothing, worthless, a complete piece of shit!"

His verbal attacks seem to hit a wall. Neither Moyer nor Mal pays him any attention. This causes a sudden change of heart, a complete flipping of emotions. Pendel feels the beads of sweat drip down from his forehead. He can't lift his arms, the pain altogether overwhelming; the sweat gets into his eyes, the sting of each bead blackening his vision temporarily.

"Look, you don't need to do this. An author goes through a lot, but violence is never the answer. You must think I'm some kind of ogre, some beast that can literally change the course of publishing, like I can actively get any editor to take a manuscript and break an author into the big time. You must think I have some kind of sway, enough clout to take your manuscript and give you what you think you deserve. And hey, even if you do deserve it, I'm just saying I can't do shit. What I wheel and deal is negotiation, impression, and reputation. All I can do is get the manuscript into the hands of editors. They are the ones that make the choices. They have to fall in love with the book, and even if they do, they still need to go to the marketing department, make a case for both the book and the author for a potentially lucrative sale. I'm just an agent; I know where the right doors are, but I can't open them."

Mal, what do you think is overwritten?

Pendel's vision returns in time to see her fingers systematically removed. Something breaks inside of him, and his mind begins to spin. Suddenly, he feels it all, the intentional sabotage he inflicted upon Mallory McAllister.

"Oh god, oh god, why? Mal. Mallory, it's true. What I did. It's all true. You were an author that I liked; your work yes, but I also liked you. I don't think I understood the extent of my feelings for you. I think it started with completely understanding the emotional depth, so dark yet honest, in your writing, and then it meshed so well with you, as a person. As my author, I became protective and then later possessive. It wasn't because I wanted to sabotage your career. I stopped giving you all that attention when I got scared. I believed that maybe I got too close, and that's one of the biggest rules an agent must abide by: Keep it all professional. I got too close and then went cold. It was me, not you. Never you. Then I couldn't stomach working on any of your projects, couldn't even speak to others about you, and when I did, I found myself speaking ill of you, as though I'd rather talk low of you. It hurt me to see that I'd choose to push one of my other authors rather than you. And when I saw that one email, you know the one, the one where you blamed me and said that you're done writing... well, I couldn't take the blame. I simply could not accept accountability. And so I made sure that your work never went anywhere. I'm sorry. I'm sorry to your fans. I'm sorry to your work. I'm sorry that *Half* didn't find a publisher. I'm so, so sorry..."

During his final and complete confession, Moyer carves away at McAllister's body, pulling bit by bit enough skin until she becomes unrecognizable. The manner with which he removes each portion, it looks as though he's practiced. This Moyer isn't acting on impulse; he has planned this, perhaps even further than Pendel could anticipate.

"I'm sorry," he says, tears welling up in his eyes. "I'm sorry..."

He can't hold on much longer, the dreamless blanket of unconsciousness culling the trauma of what he just witnessed. And then something, or rather someone, denies him that comfort. It's Moyer applying unwanted pressure to the wound.

"Apology not accepted."

Chapter 9

Pendel is in pieces; now it is my responsibility to rebuild him into a villain adequate enough for this story. The pieces are all over the hardwood floor, a body and bloodshed that amounts to something. He's going to wonder, and he's going to wither a little, and that's perfectly okay. As intended, he'll play his role.

I help him to his feet, directing him to the nearby couch. We'll have to do something about that stab wound. He winces as I position his body, arms across his chest, legs lengthened outwardly in a coffin pose.

"Good news for you," I say. "I brought everything we need to move on to the next scene." This includes a medical suture kit, disinfectant, and dressings for the wound. I make sure to show him every step, "See, I came prepared!"

There was going to be a stab wound, just like there was going to be another edit. This was the only way to get under his skin, tapping into the vein. He wouldn't have broken if I hadn't brought him to a point of regret. Look at how he acted, his full confession: Pendel had feelings for Mallory. It only takes one to win; that's what they say, right?

Agents and other confidants to an emerging author, it only

takes one! Just one editor, one person in power, to see your story and raise it to a new level.

Just like Pendel here, my agent needs just one author, one single author, to give him what he needs to not only survive but also flourish, a reputation that will glimmer and glow.

"Took you long enough," I say, knowing well that he can't speak. "Took you long enough to put the pieces together. I've been around since the initial query. You're so easy to find. Being a public figure, you're searchable, your home address, work, everything."

Pouring the disinfectant on the wound, I hold him down as he kicks and groans. The flesh around the wound has begun to change color, that trademark reddish-purple, evidence of the internal pain made physical, something he needed for a long time.

After the sting comes the relief, "Better?"

He groans.

"FYI, I've never sewn a wound shut, so cut me some slack."

There's the needle and... thread? It's so much like sewing a garment, flesh once again being merged together, forcibly becoming a single patch, a bond broken being reintroduced. I take my time with it, wiping away excess blood.

"We're going to get you back into working shape," I say.

Over, under, it all comes together. All that's left is the dressing and he's given a chance to sleep it all off. I sit there watching as he falls asleep. When he starts breathing heavily, I can't help but smile. Give him a little kiss on the forehead and then wipe away the mark. Can't be too careful. Back in the kitchen I take pictures of it, additions to my body of work. These will do nicely for the memories. Didn't get a chance to take pictures of some of the others, but thankfully the most important workshop gives me more time to settle in and enjoy the euphoria of the aftermath. His phone continues to light up, so I play the role of second assistant. Nothing I haven't done before. Some messages from an author, name doesn't matter.

"Henry, I need to talk."

When the author doesn't get a reply, they follow one text message with 15, all of them part of the world-building needed for the next act. Lots of talk about the good that Pendel did, opening doors, book deals, some film options, followed by all the minuscule fumbles, the lack of communication, the periodic stints where the author failed to hear back from Pendel. It's a damning indictment if what you find damning is utter mediocrity.

"Look, I've been talking to my friends and to my therapist and this is all giving me so much anxiety. It's really a tough decision, but I've been told that it's the right call. Given all that's coming to light, especially the article in the *New York Post* of all places, I don't think it's right not to do something, or at least say something."

Here it comes...

"I am going to make a statement on social media. It's going to say that I've made a tough decision, which it is, but I am choosing to terminate my contract."

My turn: "What are you saying?"

The sequential texts stop momentarily, the author surprised to finally receive a reply. Yet it will arrive, as plain and as simply stated as an author afraid and worried that they may never find representation ever again can make: "I'm firing you. I can't be associated. I hope you understand."

I start typing and they slip in yet another message: "But also even if you don't understand, I don't really care. I can't be seen in the same proximity as you."

My reply, terse and professional: "Understood. You'll receive a document soon. Sign it at your earliest convenience."

Got your back, Pendel. He doesn't need to see this, at least not yet.

There's a message from Marina too.

"Hey, so we've been getting a lot of emails and calls about, well, some allegations."

Jerry was the stunner, the knockout punch has everything to do with Pendel's reputation as a jackal, an ogre. He built an entire empire of favoritism, and now, those he had hurt have climbed onto the stage for their own sermon.

"Tell me," I text back.

She doesn't know it's me.

"The allegations are bad. Lots of authors and editors and even some media people are all talking about how you treated them. You… aren't coming off great."

"It's not great," I say.

She agrees, "No, it isn't."

"Thank you for letting me know." Pendel, I got your back. "Keep a list. Any confirmations thus far?"

"Confirmations?"

"Something that actually affects us?"

"I'm not sure I follow."

"Authors, contacts, that kind of thing, looking for my side of the story, looking to speak or worse, back away from us?"

"No…"

"Keep on the lookout," I say. "There may be some soon."

"You don't seem hurt by the news," she says.

"I am, but this is a business; I cannot let any emotions cloud things. Every action must be clear and deliberate."

"Okay. I guess I'm impressed."

"I know," I say, doing my best Pendel impersonation. "This is why I'm good at what I do. In the heat of a mess, I figure out how to clean things up."

Pendel passed out on the couch, I return to his side, watching him sleep.

"Whew, it all went swimmingly, didn't it?"

So be it. This author is the first, though. The first of many. One client backs away, and there will be others. By the time we reach the climax, he'll only have me. I'll have him all to myself.

Chapter 10

"Wake up. It's time for act three." Pendel comes to reclined on a couch, the pain barely present. Everything feels foggy, his arms heavy, his mouth dry. "There you are. Feeling any better? Quite the wound you got there." Pendel tries to move, finding it difficult to shift to his side. When he sees him, he panics, the lone thought being, I got to get out of here.

"She really opened you up," Moyer says. He is seated cross-legged on one of the kitchen chairs, facing him on the couch within arm's reach. Pendel tries to devise a plan of attack; if not that, a plan of escape. Where's the knife? Pendel thinks about the potential for another strike, and then it all comes apart when he remembers how it happened.

Mal.

Everything collapses. He's in tears when Moyer rests his hand on his forearm, "Sit up, let's have a chat."

What is trust when everything's at stake, the person out to get you, the very same person that wants nothing less than complete destruction of your life, your career, and your name? This has nothing to do with trust.

Moyer reads his mind, "You don't have to trust me. Better that you don't. Trust isn't going to be very valuable in the coming days and weeks."

Pendel slowly wipes the fresh tears from his eyes. He opens his mouth, but nothing comes out. He runs his tongue over his chapped lips.

"Come, sit up."

It's difficult, his body feels like dead weight, but he manages to get himself upright.

"It might help to get to know each other," says Moyer.

The thought flickers as true: *Doesn't he already know everything about me?*

"No, I don't know everything about you," he says.

Again, seemingly reading his mind.

He makes a face, causing Moyer to burst out in laughter.

"I can't read minds or whatever," he says. "That's science fiction. I'm just good at reading the scene. Call it decades of practice."

"Okay..."

Moyer uncrosses his legs and leans forward, "You should be feeling better."

He reaches for the area where he was stabbed... *where she stabbed him...*

"Careful," Moyer frowns, "Don't mess with the stitches. They're still fresh."

"That means..."

Moyer spells it out for him: "Mallory McAllister, yes. She benefited from the workshop. Frankly, I'm surprised she lasted this long. It's a good thing, though. She harbored so much resentment. An author unable to be an author... I know how she felt."

"I'm sorry," Pendel says.

"I know you are. But that doesn't change things. But let's not worry about McAllister. She was able to release it all." He points at Pendel's wound, yet again. "There's your proof. Best of all, she has helped us both. Something like this changes a person, forces them to look inward. It's been a long time coming." Moyer lets out yet another chuckle, "And if you're worrying about what will become of McAllister, she's going to be just fine."

"She's alive?"

Moyer rolls his eyes, "Come now, keep up with me. McAllister's entire oeuvre is going to be rediscovered posthumously. Every published work will be clamored over, become best sellers, and if she had written anything new, those would be ushered into publication too. But that's okay." He looks over his shoulder, causing Pendel to follow his gaze to the skeletal corpse still restrained to its chair. "They'll find her in perfect form."

Pendel cannot control his emotions, not anymore. He whimpers and begins to sob uncontrollably while Moyer does nothing to console him.

Rather, he encourages sorrow. "There you go. Feel it all. Makes for a better story."

Moyer reveals the knife, which he must know will only trigger Pendel even further. He takes great care washing it clean with a chemical. After the blade is bloodless and shiny, he sharpens it methodically, one elongated scrape after the other, before returning the weapon to its sheath. The rest of his tools are returned to the bag for safekeeping.

"What attracted you to the industry?"

It's a question so open-ended yet personal, a probe for Moyer to peer into a part of Pendel that remains unfathomable without hearing it in his own words.

So grief-stricken over the events to which he is the primary witness and accomplice, Pendel has little left to hold back. In fact, the question becomes a bastion, a temporary salve that pulls him away from all the pain to make way for nostalgia.

"I... liked to read," Pendel says.

"Yeah? Tell me more."

"I always liked a good story," Pendel exhales. "I liked how a story could transport a person into new worlds." He's suddenly bashful, self-aware, "I know, kind of hokey. But it's true. I loved escaping into books, especially when I was young. There wasn't a lot to do, and I was always sort of a loner. I had friends but I didn't get to hang out often, my mom being so strict, so I'd check out all kinds of books from the library. Didn't matter if it was too graphic or violent. I remember reading *American Psycho* when I was in, I think, sixth grade."

Moyer gets a kick out of this, offering a round of applause, "I love it."

"Yeah, I devoured books because they were the only way I could experience things. I swear it got to be so that my closest friends, the people I really knew best, were the characters in the books I kept going back to. I'd have some that I'd always reread, over and over."

"I love every part of this," says Moyer.

"Maybe it was because stories were what I confided in most, but I basically followed how books came to be. When I was in high school, I temped as a reader for a local independent publishing house. I would read and learn by doing, offering feedback that probably wasn't very useful, at least not at first, but I got better at it. I got better at it and started finding my way closer to an understanding of the publishing industry. I always knew a good story. I thrived on a good story, but then I started learning about the business of things, and it just..."

"Publishing became part of your own story."

"Yeah," Pendel nods. "Right."

"Right," Moyer grins. "Then you pursued a logical path, getting into a publishing program, and it's like they always say..."

"The rest is history," Pendel says.

"Look who's reading whose mind," says Moyer.

"What about you?" Pendel's turn to direct the spotlight. "What got you into... writing?"

"Me?" Moyer rests his hand on Pendel's wound, causing him to wince, "Oh, let's just say we're more alike than you think."

Chapter 11

Poor guy. Not that I feel sorry for him. It's like so many have said and will continue to say long after the story ends. He did this to himself. Pendel made a lot of money, forged a tremendous career, and climbed the ranks of Cooper Willis Endeavor until he became undeniably the most valuable and most influential literary agent in the business. Henry Richmond Pendel was a name of repute. Yet underneath all the big wins, he dealt in a perennial loss, this unquenchable need for validation that can only be equaled by being vilified.

And that's where I come in. He's an agent of the story, and I will ensure that he stands against the final scene as a villain nobody will ever forget.

When I see how he reacts to the remains of her body, it confirms that there still is a person beneath the jackal, the ogre, the creature to be called by many as "Pendel the Pestilence."

"Take your time," I tell him as I lead him by the hand back into the kitchen. He has expressed interest in seeing her, Mal, one last time. I told him that she's finished, her half of the story edited out. Time to move on, yet he still demanded this. *Just this once.*

I'll give it to him because I like the sound of that. It implies that he understands that there's still a long road ahead, an entirely new act. I'm going to need him receptive and willing, so yeah, I let him have his moment with the body.

Letting go of his hand, I take my seat at the head of the table.

Pendel can walk, though his body is certainly taxed by injury.

"Careful," I say, but he's not hearing me.

The guy kneels next to the body, the blood coagulating around the legs of the chair. Never mind the way this works wonders on the human senses. There's an odor, yes, but it's more than that, as if the body itself releases pheromones into the air, causing some sort of frenzy in some, and reverie in others. It jostles the memories from the dark corners of the mind, and because Pendel has a heavy heart, a lifetime of bad decisions, being at ground zero, where the story goes next, it must be tantamount to being judged by a god or a devil.

He kneels, a lifeless stare. Where are all the emotions, the grief?

The way this looks, Pendel isn't seeing the scene as-is; he looks at her so plainly dismembered and defaced, he sees not her, Mal, the person she was, but rather Mal, the author he betrayed.

Speak. He'll speak. It'll be a sort of therapy, an act of hopefully letting go, when really what I'm allowing is a moment for him to feel what it's like to take control of one's life, take control of one's emotions, and most of all, take control of all the impossible; or rather, that which you cannot control. Skim through the history of philosophy, or dive into the social sciences, and you'll see documentation about control, about chance, about all the various terminologies that get at the part of existence that continues with or without you.

"This was more about me than it was about you," he says. "I've already apologized, and I hope..." He sighs, "I hope in your dying moments you heard my apology. I guess it doesn't matter if you accepted it or not—I don't get that kind of redemption, I know—but really, I just needed to say it and believe it as truth."

I watch how he presses his palms into the blood, feeling the texture of drying blood and the way it leaves trails, brown and coppery, on the hardwood floor. Pendel brings his bloodied palm to his mouth and gives it a taste.

Good.

Keep going. Let go so that you may take control...

"My apology, to myself, has nothing to do with you." He wipes his hand against his pant leg and then rests his head on the lap of the mangled corpse, the soft yet stubbled cheek resting against the exposed femur. "Really, it's the idea of you. My author. You were my author, and it drove me crazy that I couldn't get you the best deal possible. I couldn't steer you toward the more commercial sale, the better book... I couldn't even guide you to the better idea. I couldn't even maintain a professional relationship. It was the thought that I wasn't doing my job, and by not doing my job, it was the worry that I would be found out as an imposter."

At some point, it becomes clear to me that he isn't talking to her, not to Mal. No, can't be. He addresses all his authors. He addresses everything as though he once believed that he could manifest the world for anyone who decided to take his side.

"Manifest, they say, what you want, not what you worry you'll become... That's why I did what I did to you. That's why I continue to pounce when I see a potential payday. And that's why I often can't help myself; I see a fire and I want to stoke the flames. Sometimes it involves a bit of jealousy; mostly, and I know why now, it's because I'd rather have control over you than no control at all."

Breakthrough, we have ourselves another valiant step forward!

Poor guy. Pendel looked for control in the wrong places. Now he's lost more, even less of a firm grip on his life and career. He won't be able to hold on much longer, but that's okay: He's found his next biggest client, and he's going to change everything.

This is how leaders of cults and countries find themselves at the helm of impossible power, and it's also how those very same beings lose sight of themselves to give into oblivion.

But not Pendel.

At least, not until I'm done with him.

How'd that song go again? I can't remember the rhythm...

Poor guy. He probably thinks this story's about him.

Chapter 12

Truly awake for possibly the first time in years, Pendel can think clearly. The weight and pressure were so commonplace that he had grown used to it, fully adapted to high stress and high anxiety. Now there's nothing left, not really, save for the final, mandatory acceptance.

This is what Moyer offers. This is what Pendel hears. A transactional event to establish the end of one act and the beginning of another.

Pendel takes his seat at the other end of the table.

He and Moyer gaze at each other, both waiting for the other to speak. Moyer reaches into the same bag full of murderous instruments and produces a bound manuscript. He sets it carefully onto the table and slides it over to Pendel.

Printed in CAPS is the title FRIENDS SELLING FRIENDS, the same book that Pendel had rejected weeks, maybe months, before. Yet it isn't the title or the novel itself that is of any use or urgency, evidence of such being in how the title has been crossed out multiple times.

"Read the pages," Moyer says.

It's a request.

"Please."

Not at all a demand.

"Just the first few."

This is a meeting of two parties, a most pivotal event because in theory, an author being read is a vulnerable act.

Of course, Pendel is compelled to at least see what awaits; what must a story written using vitriol, a story written with a knife and a need for vengeance look like on the page? He starts reading. From sentence one, he experiences a young talent, a glimpse of Alexander Moyer before he had his breakthrough. Turning the page, he sees new edits done in red ink. In places, the pen must have begun leaking because red speckle dashes the margins, bleeds across the end of paragraphs. Chapter one ends with the entire last graph crossed out, the edit in the margins reads: *Are you willing to do anything?*

This is Moyer's confession, as much as he is willing to reveal. The vulnerable act, he offers the massacre of his novel, the work he put everything into, sacrificing friendships and career opportunities to align his path with the romanticized notion of the author. Dead-end jobs, meager living situations, packaging all amounts of time as exclusive to sitting alone in a room with nothing more than his thoughts, research, laptop, blinking cursor, and the latest novel demand. *Friends Selling Friends* represents what was lost. The body next to him represents his breakthrough, the latest in a most unique body of work.

Yes, Moyer is willing to do anything.

Pendel reads another chapter, noting more speckle and splatter, writing in the margins that has little to do with the novel itself. They speak to the agent, ask open-ended questions about the industry: Offering representation, what does that even imply? Why is it called a submission, like it's inherently an act of weakness and subservience? Why P&Ls when everyone knows that no two books are alike? Authors marketing themselves... what happened to publishers supporting their authors?

He looks up from the page, catching sight of a sly look on Moyer's face.

"What do you think?"

A wince, the painkillers starting to wear off, "It's off to a good start."

"That's not what an author really wants to hear, you know?"

"You're an author," Pendel says. No question about it, yet saying it aloud jostles free an additional association that Pendel had not viewed as valid. Moyer the stalker. Moyer the serial killer. Moyer the psychopath. Moyer the worst thing that's happened to him. But never: Moyer the emerging author. Yet there it is now, and to further let it sink in, Moyer slides a laminated sheet of paper, which just barely makes it to Pendel's end of the table. He gazes down at it and understands immediately what he's seeing.

A one-sheet, typically designed to accompany a prepress review copy of a book, yet here, Moyer has generated one for himself. The written copy mentions nothing about his book.

"I laminated it, just in case you tried to tear it up before reading it fully," says Moyer.

Instead, it explains Pendel's worst nightmare. Ego death, destruction of reputation. It's everything he doesn't want to believe, yet it's everything that can surely come to pass. In two paragraphs, Moyer tells a little story involving Pendel's dissolution of his client list by way of a mass author exodus. Every author fires him, and many editors refuse to speak to, much less work with Pendel. There's a sentence discussing how he sues for defamation, but it backfires, leading to more negative press. The copy so plainly explains his demise that it doesn't even feel like anything; the one sheet washes over Pendel like any other of its type. It's theoretical, offering a possibility, nothing more. After the copy there's the sole market log line, identical to the question posed in the margins of Moyer's dead manuscript: "Are you willing to do anything?"

The blurbs are a venerable cluster of recognizable names:

"You don't have to do this."
—J.D. Church

"I just wanted to connect."
—Brendon Kawada

"*cries for help*"
—Chelsea Boll

"There's no going back once you start."
—Mallory McAllister

And Pendel quickly recognizes what they all have in common. There, at the bottom, Alexander Moyer, a writer and emerging author of... a three-sentence bio, succinct, offering some solid bylines like the *London Review*.

"Isn't it beautiful?" Moyer says. "Now that I got your attention, you'll see that there is still something. I mean, you're fucked. Don't get me wrong. But there's still something beyond the public trials and tribulations that will come barreling toward you. There's something you can control, and it may be the very thing that saves you from everything."

"What... are you talking about?" He thinks about it and then asks, "What is it?"

"Me," he says, matter-of-factly.

Everything's right there on the table. Pendel flips through the manuscript, gives the one-sheet a second look, and then nods, "Okay."

"Great!" Moyer says, walking over to him, retrieving both the manuscript and the one-sheet. He takes the documents to the kitchen sink and starts a fire, feeding it with the dead manuscript and the dead truth.

"What do we do with..." It's how Pendel says "*we*" and so quickly takes his place at Moyer's side, the subservient one, his turn to exist in the shadows of an entirely different jackal and ogre.

"Oh, Mal," he shrugs. "They'll find her, eventually."

After the documents are turned to ash and flushed down the drain with water, Moyer moves on with the next steps. "Come, help me," he says. "Help me, and you help yourself. Either your story ends with a ruined reputation and jail time, or the establishment of infamy and a reputation as a serial killer." Moyer hands him a scrubber and some bleach, "You've made your choice, so come, be a good killer and help me rid the scene of all fingerprints."

Chapter 13

On the ride back into Manhattan, I'm telling him about my process. Pendel's already proving to be a good accomplice, asking me all kinds of questions, making me feel like he cares about my work. I'm finding this undivided attention addicting, something you never realize you enjoy so much until you experience it firsthand. Confiding in someone backed into a corner is a unique opportunity. We stick to a low whisper, starting from the top.

"You went for Jerry first," he says. "How did you make the decision?"

"Taking a life isn't easy, I'll give you that, and worse when it's someone that's so recognizable. He's always got extra eyes on him." I think about the question, shocked that I hadn't given it much thought. "I didn't choose Jerry; he chose me. He's on social media and he's always posting where he is. I was able to follow his every stop on the tour, every visit. When he arrived in New York City, I was waiting for him at the JetBlue terminal at JFK."

"He didn't even tell me when he was arriving," says Pendel.

"I'm good at what I do," I say.

He leans in close, "Had you taken a life prior to Jerry?"

Just have to know everything, huh?

I shake my head, "Nope. My first."

"Wow."

"It all started coming to me after so much rejection. You sit in this horrible feeling that it's never going to work out for you, and it starts to blind you from who you are as a person. The feeling you can't ever shake." I look at him and can tell he doesn't understand. "Look, imagine if you couldn't get your business into the black, unable to make any money, despite having that eye for talent? No matter what you did, you couldn't find the right clients, they all sign with other agents, and you couldn't make enough to keep the lights on."

Then again, he's going to find out what it's like very soon...

"Horrible," he says. "Just horrible."

"I felt this way for a long time. After you passed, things kind of fell apart. I went a little mad. Nothing mattered. Then one day I found myself reading about the trade publishing industry. Countless interviews and testimony in various court cases, publishing horror stories and even Poets & Writers advice columns. I became a scholar of the industry."

"This industry can drive a person to kill," he nods.

"The more I learned, the closer I got to my breakthrough."

"Jerry," he says.

"You could say that." I notice someone eavesdropping, a look of concern on his face. I turn and say, "I'm an author." It's enough to make him lose interest, believing all that's being said is the mere process of getting the words on the page.

"Anyway, I saw it all unfold, my body of work already plotted out, one scene after the other, and it was there, just waiting for me to follow through. You set them all up, and I ensured that they would become a name. When I'm done, everyone, especially those in the industry, will never forget any of their names." I flash him a grin, "Especially you. You're going to be remembered."

He looks out the window, "I would have liked to be known for being a great agent."

"The thing about that is..."

Pendel brushes it off, "I know. I didn't exactly help myself with my behavior. When you're at the top, it's easy to forget that the fall is twice as deadly." He asks me another question, "Didn't you ever, I don't know, hesitate?"

Again, the answer can only be no. "I didn't, no. Hearing them beg, it's infectious. It's such a rush. Besides, I'm the one there to make the save. I'm saving them. Every single workshop, I make it clear where they are as an author, critiquing their craft, helping them meet their true potential."

"True potential," he says, like an echo.

"You were a special guest. You saw how I work."

"I certainly did," he sighs.

"Cheer up," I say, giving him a nudge. "Not all is lost. In fact, you got your biggest find right here." I give him a wink. "Right?"

It sinks in, what I'm implying. Understanding that he's got no choice at all, he holds onto the fear, the sheer trepidation, and plays along. "Yes. You'll be bigger than Jerry."

"Don't compare your authors," I say, scolding him. "One of the many reasons things aren't blowing over for you."

"You're right," he says.

The train comes to a stop. We're almost there.

"You tell Marina yet?"

"No, not yet," he says.

"That's okay. I already did."

"What?"

Oh, come on. He's got to stop pretending. Let go and accept.

"This is what I do, Pendel. You need to accept reality. You need to accept that I am in control of everything. She knows you've signed a new author, just like she knows that you've lost a few. Marina's in the know. She probably has a better sense of the industry than you do."

Letting out a sigh, he seems to agree, "Then you've already signed the paperwork?"

"Where do you think we're going right now?" I lean back in my seat, "There's still more to the day. By this time tomorrow, you'll be an entirely different person."

He isn't listening, instead he asks me again, "But how can you... *kill* a person?"

"Hey, keep up with me," I say, slapping him across the face.

The sound turns some heads, makes Pendel feel like even less. I lean in and whisper, "It's about sacrifice. You have to make sacrifices if you want to be the best at your craft. The way this story goes, I need more than a few sacrificial characters. Authors make it easy; they want so much validation that they'll often take part in their own destruction." I watch a couple arguing on the train platform. "And to answer your question, I think of how miserable they already are. It makes the kill easier. You're saving them from themselves."

The train starts moving, next stop, Penn Station.

I clap my hands together and shout, "Let's make it official!"

Chapter 14

Marina is surprised to see him. Most of the other employees have already left the office, leaving Pendel and Moyer to use the bigger conference room, all in private. Marina keeps the information to herself, but it's looking like Pendel's time at the agency will soon come to an end. To sign a new author right now isn't a good look, and more so a poor business decision. Yet that's the thing about Pendel: He does what he wants.

Pendel is putting on an act. He never acts this happy to see her, or anyone for that matter. He masks everything in a false sense of amiability, "Marina, meet Alex. Alex, meet Marina. This is the new author I'm signing. He's going to be huge!" Another slip-up, measuring his authors with a constant ruler of judgment. "She's my assistant. What would I do without her?"

Moyer is led into Pendel's office, where the agency contract is already on his desk, waiting for their signatures.

Marina stands at the doorway, refusing to take part in the meeting.

Pendel insists, "Sit down. You'll want to get to know Alex."

Pendel sits behind his desk, grabs a pen, and signs the contract. "Your turn."

Moyer uses the same pen, signing on the line with a laugh. "I used to dream of this moment. It felt different in my imagination, more monumental."

"Yeah well, it's just business," Marina chimes in, gathering the documents.

"I said you're staying," says Pendel, eying her attempt to flee the scene. To Moyer, he says, "Well then, welcome to the team."

"Thanks," says Moyer. "It's great to know that I've found my champion."

"Hey Marina, this guy writes some of the best murders in the entire business. The way he just goes for it, full detail, sparing the reader no relief, it's impressive."

"Thanks," Moyer grins. This is the point of the meeting: Give the author complete and unadulterated validation. Upon signing, the new author must feel like they are on top of the world. Anything they want, the sky's the limit. "It took me so many years, honing my craft. You know the drill. I sucked for a long time until I had my big breakthrough. Suddenly I knew what kind of story I wanted to tell. The rest just fell into place."

"Uh huh," Pendel, all fake grins and nods. "Tell her about your work."

Moyer looks over his shoulder, "Really...?"

"Yeah, go right ahead. Tease her with a story. She'll love it."

Moyer begins by explaining what sounds like a book, a thriller. Marina listens, expecting it to be the manuscript she read but Pendel rejected, *Friends Selling Friends,* yet the details sound completely different.

"The first person to perish, he's flying into the city, you know, because he's a big deal, has a lot of fans, and is there to do some events. The killer waits for him at the terminal and then follows him to the hotel. At the hotel, he pays extra to get the room right next to the guy. They have this little back and forth in the hallway, just the cute and adorable stuff you'd expect when the 'biggest fan' meets their hero."

He describes a murder spree in a city, yet all the details are missing, save for the graphic detail of each kill. Marina has trouble making sense of it.

"It's later that there's a knock on the door. Little mistakes,"

Moyer snaps his finger. "It's always the little mistakes that become life-threatening. The guy ends up in the hotel room, able to completely carve up the body."

Pendel is all smiles, nodding like he approves, stopping Moyer only to ask for even more detail. "Wait, talk about how it smells, the insides of a human stomach."

Moyer chuckles, "If you think vomit smells bad, just wait until you smell the stomach acids and partially digested food."

More laughter. Moyer starts talking about a night in the park, another victim meeting their demise. "Blood doesn't stay warm for very long," he explains. "And don't get me started on the texture of blood when it starts to dry."

"Tell us about that one scene," Pendel says, searching for specifics. "What was it, the one at the kitchen table."

"Oh right," Moyer says. "The one where the victim wants to die and tells the killer how to cut herself up."

"Yeah!"

Moyer turns to Marina and grins, "I had to do some research for that one. So much can be found on the internet, but some details you just have to see to believe."

Marina begins to feel queasy.

"Stop," she says, eventually. "I think I'm going to be sick."

Pendel and Moyer both laugh.

"See? So evocative," Pendel says.

"Thank you," Moyer says, enjoying yet another compliment.

"You're going to mess with people's minds," Pendel says.

"I'm going to make them second guess the system."

"Yes! You're going to make them think twice about tradition and trade. You're going to have them thinking about those scenes, the entire story, for months to come," Pendel says.

"And isn't that what it's all about? Leaving a mark. Making people wake up and take notice? There's a fatal flaw to every single business, everything on this earth. I think what I'm doing, why I'm doing it, is to make people wake up and think. I want them to second guess what seems so ironclad. I want them to see that if there's any hierarchy, it can't be good. It's probably a house of cards waiting to fall over."

It's a showing, two actors doing their best. This is all part of the story, and this scene's important. It's the moment when both villain and victim choose oblivion.

Pendel with yet another compliment, "You're going to have a long, acclaimed, bestselling career. I suspect we're going to be working together for a long time."

"I'm just happy to be here," he says.

"Marina, ask him a question," says Pendel. "I bet you have plenty."

"Umm," she clears her throat. "Well..."

"Don't be shy," Pendel says.

"Yeah," Moyer nods. "I'm an open book."

She defaults to a common question, one nearly every author is asked, particularly by those in the industry: "How did you endure so many years of rejection?"

Moyer shrugs, "We all have a story to tell. Some are just willing to do anything to tell it."

Part Four
DEAL OF THE DAY

Chapter 1

It feels good, having representation. *My agent.* I finally have the capability to possess and be possessed. My agent, my author: We're both going to be remembered for this.

Shortly after one author drops Pendel, there are more. The current count is something like 12. I ask him how many clients he has but he won't answer. Really, he isn't the right person to turn to in times of need. That's why I've got Marina, who sends me the agent directory, a list totaling over 200 names. I'm not quite sure if the number should come as a surprise. How many clients must an agent have to survive?

Anyway, Pendel is counting on me. I tell him to sleep this off. His apartment is so deafeningly quiet in the early morning hours, aided by it facing a courtyard rather than the busy avenue. He's cocooned in blankets, snoring loudly; the guy hasn't left his office since Jerry bled out. He's going to need some energy for what's about to happen.

To help him out, I field all correspondence.

This is all to be expected. Pendel in the spotlight for the wrong reasons has many of his clients worried. About an hour ago, the *New York Post* published an article detailing what they call "a mass exodus" of clientele from the "formerly leading agent." A bit premature, but this is what I expected. I couldn't have fully predicted the rollout, but it was evident that he'd lose clients. Authors are the skittish type, too afraid of how they'll be viewed by the public to stand by their agent.

The article is substantial. There are four authors named, each getting their own Google search. I should know their names; they may end up part of the story. I really should have worked on getting another byline. In honor of Mal, I decided against it. Her work will find its way, just as I will find out who poached these authors, and what they've sold.

The name Violet Blue sounds familiar. A quick search yields a bunch of porn sites. Right, the porn star. She's known for her girl-girl bondage flicks, and according to a fan site dedicated to collecting every photo and video, she has since become a top 10 porn star on OnlyFans.

In the article, she is quoted as saying, "Pendel was always responsive and kind enough, to me at least, until he got what he wanted." Once again, his pattern of behavior is made apparent: favoritism and grooming, manipulation of minds, and a predilection for pitting his authors against each other. "He sold a book and then I never heard back from him," she says. "Well, he'd only ever email me about foreign rights or something like that."

To the credit of the journalist, they did a decent job vetting the claims. They wrote this article with a sense of objectivity that is frankly uncommon for a site like the *New York Post.*

Her official website is all pornography, so I tweak my search terms so that I get more information about the book Pendel sold. It's a collection of short stories titled *Shades of Blue*, published last year by FSG. Looking at the Goodreads page, and then Amazon, the book seems to have done well enough. 3.9 rating average across 8k reviews. BookScan numbers show that it sold just under 19k. That's good, I believe, though what is considered "good sales" is determined on a book-by-book basis, often compared to the P&L document... that is if anybody actually ever goes back to that thing once a book is bought.

I don't have to look very hard to find out who signed her,

clearly tagged in her byline on Instagram. It looks like her new agent already sold a book, this time a memoir.

Adult film star **Natasha "Violet Blue" McNamara**'s **ALL THEY SEE IS BLUE**, an autobiographical novel about her experiences in the adult film industry, written in the form of her brand, depicting each scene and kink through the industry's portrayal of the female body, to **Hendrix de Leon** at **Alfred A. Wolf**, in a preempt, by **Jenny Jacobs** at **Writer's House** (NA).

There's the name I'm looking for.

Hendrix. Seems he is undeterred by the events surrounding his most prized and closest agent. Searching Publishers Marketplace, the number is right there: Pendel's sold 37 books to Hendrix. 37. That's an important number for this story. Pendel would have done the same for Emily Mills, the same for any editor who stroked his ego and gave him everything he wanted.

Author Tad Davidson is quoted in the article too. Pretty cool. I had no idea that Pendel represented the author. He has written some good crime fiction. Davidson only has the one quote, "I was always suspicious of how Pendel could turn things around in mere minutes, like he held all the strings and knew which ones to pull."

Not so much a damning statement as it is yet another hint at Pendel's stranglehold over the publishing industry. Searching his name, I see that he's also sold something:

Victor award-winning author **Tad Davidson**'s **KISS AND TELL**, is about an alcoholic detective facing possible murder charges called upon by his former friend and hot-shot DEA enforcer to come out of his hermetic bubble for one last case, involving a deadly organized crime syndicate that deals in sex trafficking and drugs, to **Greg Doas** at **Kessinger**, in a major deal, by **Michael Oliver** at **Vermillion and Co.** (NA).

The other two authors named both say the same thing: Pendel made them feel small. It's the anonymous authors who implicate Pendel for illicit and borderline illegal business dealings.

Emerging arts fellow and star of the critically acclaimed documentary on homelessness *A Hard Place*, **Kyle Rubin**'s **PARENTHESIS**, a debut novel about the area of space between statements, featuring twin protagonists on opposite ends of the justice system, one an attorney and another a lobbyist, both seeking the truth from a country dealing exclusively in lies, to **Karl Smith** at **HRH**, in a preempt, by **William Carth** at **The Anderson Agency** (NA).

All these authors call harm and foul, yet by the looks of it, they're all doing more than fine.

Debut novelist **Hayden Feehan**'s **OLIVE BRANCH**, a multi-generational family saga set around managing a failing vineyard, and **COLOR SWATCH**, a short story collection of culinary and linguistics in equal measure, to **Forsythe Monahan** at **Chronicle Books**, in a preempt, by **Heather Ann Augusto** at **Inkling** (World).

One agent's demise is another agent's hot hand. For everyone that leaves Pendel, it appears they are given a clean slate; best of all, all this publicity yields attention to all manuscripts out on submission.

This is reputation death.

By the time he's speaking to hopeful authors at the Iowa Writer's Workshop, there will be a drastic shift in his public persona. In the audience, his demons will sit in wait, dormant until he speaks up and is put under the spotlight.

To get there, we're going to need to make a dire statement.

Thankfully I have both office and cell numbers. I also have his home address. Lives in Sunset Park in a nice part of the neighborhood. Hendrix de Leon, we're going to work through this. By the time we're done, he'll become a pivotal part of the story.

Don't you worry, Henry. You're in good hands.

Chapter 2

He wakes up to the detective's call. Pendel was so exhausted, he fell into a heavy, dreamless sleep. Barely able to shake free the clouds of slumber, he reaches for the phone and answers, "Hello?" Wasting no time, Detective Monroe's tone has drastically changed. Where he had once been competitive yet overall courteous, it has all been tossed aside. In its place, he has no reason not to treat Pendel like the monster he believes him to be.

"Check social media," the detective says.

"Excuse..."

"Shut up. Check social media."

Pendel rubs his eyes, lowering the phone receiver only to realize the call was made to his landline, not his cell phone. A moment's hesitation, he blinks and slowly comes to the reality of what's happened during his brief slumber.

He finds his cell phone on the bedside table, plugged in and charging. Countless notifications keep the phone scalding hot, the screen ever glowing. He ignores the texts, the calls, though one pokes through, a familiar industry publication, *The Bookseller*, likely calling for a quote, yet another article about Pendel in the works. He goes to social media, notices that his notifications have maxed out, the sheer vitriol being thrust his way. Pendel looks and sees that his name is trending. Clicking PENDEL leads to a viral post by the *New York Post*. Its contents surmise the end of Pendel's career, calling it a "mass exodus" of clients choosing to leave Pendel and Cooper Willis Endeavor.

"You see it?"

Pendel clears his throat, "Yeah. Yeah, I see it."

"Good, now are you going to tell me the truth, or are you going to make this difficult?"

He's skimming through the article, noting the names quoted. Damn, they got Davidson? He had always liked Tad's writing. What's more, Tad sold books. Lots of books. He was always an easy name to represent, the submission window ever short and offers usually rolled in within a week.

Pendel's mind has trouble processing everything that's happened. The detective doesn't give him a chance to speak, quickly darting off new details, "I was willing to keep my mind open, even when it was odd that every single victim happened to be one of your authors. I've seen some crazy shit on the job. Nothing is ever as it seems. But then you came along, and I disliked you from the moment we first met. Every detective learns quickly to trust a first impression. My first impression, it wasn't good, Pendel. You came off as a crook, a shady presence so full of himself I really wanted to find a reason to book you right then and there." Detective Monroe raises his voice, "But you just backed yourself into a corner, Pendel. You just can't help yourself, can you?"

"I..."

The detective doesn't let him speak, "Nope, I gave you a shot. You had your chance to confess, to explain yourself. But you just play stupid, fine, do that. What you ought to do is get your ass down to the precinct right fucking now so that I can arrest you and be done with this media circus! Oh, but no, you won't play easy. You'd rather make this obnoxious..."

"That's not true," Pendel says.

The detective isn't listening, "No, you're clearly getting off on this shit. You love the attention, even if it's being a public enemy. Well, you have your fun, okay?! You have your fun, but the moment you slip up, the moment I have the evidence to take you down, you're going down. And you are never, ever going to know what it feels like to have freedom ever again! You'll be filed away in some shitty jail cell where there's barely any light, and you'll waste away, alone and miserable. That, I assure you, is your future!"

"You have to let me explain," Pendel says. "This isn't what—"

"Nope, unless you're going to confess, I'm done playing nice. Once I get that one piece of evidence, you're finished. Life **over**."

The call ends, Pendel left completely stunned.

"Was that Monroe?" Moyer appears at the foot of his bed, arms crossed. Had he been listening the entire time?

Pendel drops the receiver and yawns, "Yeah."

"He suspects something," Moyer says.

Another nod. "Yup."

"I'd advise you not to feed him any details. He's hot on the trail, but unless you confess or we mess up, he has nothing but suspicion and a bunch of online controversy to feast on."

He's still making sense of the latest developments, particularly the so-called "mass exodus." A tinny beeping can be heard coming from the receiver. Pendel picks it up and places it back on its source. "Did Tad Davidson really fire me?"

Moyer takes a tentative step toward the right side of his bed, "Davidson, Violet Blue, Kyle Rubin..." He trails off and then snaps his fingers, remembering the name, "Hayden Feehan."

"Hayden Feehan," Pendel sighs. "I don't know a Hayden Feehan."

Moyer laughs, "Were you always this forgetful?"

What can he really say? Yes, no? Pendel hasn't made peace with the fact that his selective memory is self-manifested. How can one remember a name if they never bothered to hear it in the first place?

"I don't know," he says.

"You do," Moyer chuckles. "The only reason why you remember my name is because I made it evident and clear. If you were tested, I bet you couldn't name more than a handful of your clients."

No comment.

"Thought so," Moyer says.

"Should I feel bad about what's happening?"

Moyer's turn to shrug it off, "Don't know. Up to you. It makes no difference for the story. Your place in the narrative is defined well enough. No need for edits."

Pendel scans the room, for what? Anything. A sense of solvency, something that reminds him that he still has some control over his life. Failing to find it, his attention returns to Moyer, who paces around the room. There it is, the sense he needed, found in his new signee, *my author*. A note of confidence, helping Pendel believe that maybe, just maybe, there is a future where he doesn't end up in jail.

"No time to waste," Moyer says. He walks over to Pendel's closet and retrieves clothing: a shirt, blazer, and dress pants. He glimpses the tie rack and selects one. "They're circling like sharks, but we're a few steps ahead. They'll find her soon; by then we need to be a few chapters into the story."

Mal.

"Yup," Moyer says, reading his mind. "They're going to find Mal. Either the postal worker or her family, probably her daughter, who tends to come home first. They'll find her and it'll quickly be linked to your client list. Meaning, they'll continue to chase after you."

"You need to help me," Pendel pleads.

Moyer tosses the clothes onto the bed, "Duh. You can count on me. I know how this story ends."

Chapter 3

He's full of ideas, but I'm not going to ask. There's only one editor that comes to mind. When I tell Pendel what needs to happen next for the story to truly hit its peak, that perfect and provocative climax, we need to move from authors to editors. He has a whole list of editors he hates, but no, I don't think so.

"Hush now," I tell him. "The answer is right there, at the top of your inbox."

Hendrix. It must be Hendrix.

The history between agent and author, dozens of book deals yielding a sudden betrayal, Hendrix backing away from Pendel in a show of trepidation and disgust: It's still a betrayal, and one that establishes motive. Why wouldn't Pendel be upset? Hendrix had been backing away from the agent for months, long before the news broke of Pendel's poor behavior.

It kind of gets you thinking, how did he know before everybody else? Yeah, think about it for more than a second and Hendrix becomes increasingly more suspicious. It's almost like he knew before everybody else. And who really would have handed him that kind of information?

I wonder.

Let me tell you about Hendrix. As previously mentioned, he

was once a young and ambitious editor, an assistant to a long-retired editor. When he started at Alfred A. Wolf, he was fresh, wide-eyed, the kind of employee that gets exploited by the disaffected and desensitized long-standing employees. He, too, went to the Columbia Publishing Course. Just like Pendel... and just like Pendel, he found his way into the industry through a genuine interest in reading.

He wanted to be a part of the story. Not an author himself, he found a role as an editor, helping sculpt the story. And an editor is someone who learns by doing, similar to an author. An emerging editor cuts their teeth on the slush, the hefty and dreary act of reading submissions, offering that feedback, and slowly but surely becoming someone who has the right eye.

Hendrix gets this email one day. It's not really a submission, not exactly. Rather, it's a recognizable name, Henry Richmond Pendel. The agent reaches out to offer Hendrix his congratulations. You see, Pendel saw the job move on Publishers Marketplace. Hendrix is promoted to associate editor, which means he has the newfound responsibility of acquiring a select number of books. Pendel earned his reputation as being the first and the best, there to forge a new transactional relationship the moment anyone becomes of value to him.

Hendrix is just shy of his 26th birthday when he is promoted.

The email is overwhelming for such a young editor. Its contents depict what Pendel does best, doting out a sizable helping of positivity, making the recipient feel not only welcomed but also high on validation. Pendel is keen to point out Hendrix's meteoric rise, how every manuscript he read and offered positive feedback went on to be successful books, all of them selling better than expected. Pendel makes sure to keep the door open, building Hendrix up to be his next toy, confidant, and inside editor who can meet the demands he requires.

That's how it started, with a nice email. From that point on, there wasn't a day that Hendrix didn't receive an email. The way it starts, talking about upcoming books and what Hendrix is looking for, to the eventual manipulation into prioritizing Pendel's submissions over other agents. It wasn't all that shocking; Hendrix was impressionable. He wanted to be seen as a valuable editor. Most importantly, and not to be discounted: He felt the pressure to produce successful books. If an author is only as good as their last book, then an editor has twice the pressure, for their primary role is to ensure that a book is in the best shape before entering production.

Hendrix is lulled into a degree of confidence by the quality of Pendel's submissions. After so many hits, the backchannel between agent and editor became ironclad.

Pendel could sell whatever he wanted to Hendrix, and Hendrix would buy anything from Pendel in a heartbeat. It was a professional bond tantamount to insider trading… yet what nobody else knew didn't hurt them, right?

Pendel's pattern of behavior…

How did Hendrix know?

Thing about getting the story right, you need to be thorough with your research. You need to seek every corner, every option, and in this case, I needed to meet the editor who ushered in some of the most lucrative deals for both the publishing house and Pendel.

He's easy to find, you see. Scheduled for an informational meeting, posing as a journalist interested in profiling Hendrix. I make sure to have the meeting in his office, so I'm aware of the details and whereabouts of an editor when it comes time for the story to include him.

That morning, I show up as a journalist, and it's unmemorable. Our interactions are made to be intentionally blasé, the usual 20 questions. Yet I see how he reacts to being in the spotlight; I notice how Hendrix has adopted some qualities from Pendel. His ego has been inflated, his understanding of where he rests currently in the internal hierarchy at Alfred A. Wolf renders him borderline indulgent in all things personal accolades. It's easy to talk him up while I tell him everything he needs to know about his favorite agent.

He learns about the favoritism.

He learns about the grooming.

He learns about Jerry and Pendel's predatory behavior.

He learns about Mallory McAllister.

He learns about everything, and then I'm the one that puts him on the spot, "In light of these allegations, and having worked closely with the agent, would you like to comment on your professional relationship with Henry Richmond Pendel?"

It's enough to scare an editor so reliant upon his reputation. It's where both he and Pendel are identical. Of course, a question like that, after so many easy ones, I'm not getting any straight answers. He's flustered, for sure, but my research is complete. That morning, I did the groundwork. I gathered all the necessary research, learned about the most important and precious editor, and found the inspiration I needed. Best of all, the editor knew first, even before the agent. He always said he wanted to be part of the story.

Well...

Hendrix, your wish is about to be granted.

Chapter 4

No need to search very hard to find Hendrix. Moyer briefs Pendel on Hendrix's routines, and after some coercion, the agent agrees to go along. Better yet, Moyer talks him into taking the lead. "Infamy," says Moyer, whenever Pendel hesitates. Hendrix, it turns out, is a workaholic just like Pendel. You can find him in his office every day, well after hours. When they make the commute to the Alfred A. Wolf offices, it's a little after 8:30 PM on a Monday, typically an hour of the evening when only some of the assistants remain hustling and working to break even, to catch their breath. Hendrix is drowning in submissions, to-do list items.

They find him in his office, head down, face inches from his computer screen. His short hair looks slightly unkempt. If they bothered to pry, they'd discover that Hendrix had spent much of the day going through backlists, cross-checking rights and contractual obligations for many of Pendel's now ex-clients. Hendrix received an order from publisher Jonathan Sharpe to inspect the contracts for any foul play, see if they can renegotiate with the authors' new agents.

Lights are off, all is quiet.

The nearest employee is on the other end of the eighth floor, busily collating and working through some past-due proofs.

"You know what to do," Moyer says.

"Wait, you're not..."

Moyer chooses to stand back, hidden by the shadows, a situation of comfort and reassurance after years of standing aside.

"If you have any trouble, just remember what he did."

Betrayal. Can Pendel find enough hurt in his heart to take a life?

It must be more than taking a life, though. Moyer hands over his bag full of various items, murderous utensils, all vetted from previous workshops.

Tonight, an agent meets with an editor to make some key changes to the story as it currently stands. There can only be one that survives the night; for the story to work, one must die. Pendel pauses every few steps, expecting Hendrix to look up from his screen and notice him standing there in the hallway.

He gets a free pass. The story demands that he hurt this man, bleed him out slowly, give him enough feedback to never again betray the hand that feeds.

Hendrix is too busy to see Pendel at his office door, stepping inside and closing the blinds. He's too slow to react to Pendel's swift inceptive moves, namely the quick draw of the knife, the hasty dash toward Hendrix's desk, and the preemptive blade against his neck.

"Pendel?! The fuck?"

Pendel wants to end this quickly, pushing the blade firmly against the soft flesh of Hendrix's neck.

"You've gone mad," says Hendrix.

This is it; all he needs to do is drag the blade firmly across, dig deep enough to let the lifeblood pour out, and then it can all be over. Yet as one moment passes, and in another gasp, Hendrix is fighting back, grabbing at the blade, shouting for help. Pendel's slight hesitation threatens to ruin the entire story.

Moyer walks into the office, locking the door.

He sighs, "Really?"

Pendel loosens his grip, Hendrix falling to the floor, crawling around the desk, taking solace in a corner. He gazes up at Moyer and plays his part, "Who, who the fuck are you?!"

"You can do better," says Moyer. Then he looks down at Hendrix, "You both can. 'Who the fuck are you?' Is that the best you can do? How many years editing manuscripts and the best you can do when facing your enemy, is to pretend you don't recognize me? Or even attempt to understand why Henry would maybe want to end your life?"

Hendrix presses his hand against his neck, checking for any blood loss, and then says, "I didn't think Pendel would go off the deep end."

"He's lucid, knows where the story's going," Moyer says. "Isn't that right, Henry?"

Henry won't say a word. His moment has passed, a failure.

Hendrix checks his hand, sees no blood, and then chuckles, "You really shouldn't have done that, Pendel. I mean, I understand that you're going through a lot right now..." Hendrix returns to his desk, leans back in his chair, seemingly not at all worried about his safety, "But you got to admit that you did this to yourself? Jesus Christ, Henry, pitting your authors against each other?! The thing with Jerry?! This isn't good. No good at all! How can you not understand my need to distance myself from you?"

Moyer retrieves the bag from Pendel. He offers a suggestion, "What makes you think you can still get away?"

"Excuse me," Hendrix says. "But I don't know who you think you are, but I've had enough of this shit. I'm going to get back to this, okay? Pendel, you get the fuck out of here. I never want to hear from you again. Hear me? You too."

"Hear you loud and clear," says Moyer. In his right hand, he holds a hammer, which still looks brand-new, and has a price tag affixed to its handle. Moyer launches his body over the desk, driving the claw of the hammer into Hendrix's eyes. The left eye gouged, Hendrix's bloodcurdling screams, yet Moyer is not quite satisfied. "Ugh, this is no good." He inspects the hammer, clearly his intention was to gouge both eyes. He shakes his head, snaps a look at Pendel, "I'm not happy. This all needs to be edited out."

"Can't you just..." Pendel can't say the words.

A knock on the door. "Umm, hello?"

Must be the production assistant.

Moyer drives the face of the hammer into Hendrix's skull repeatedly until the screams stop. Hendrix's face is unrecognizable. They both remain silent until they hear the assistant's footsteps walking away.

He shakes his head, looking at the mess.

The manner of Hendrix's demise, it doesn't make sense, not for the story. There's no emphasis on betrayal, no use of a callback. Instead, what they have is a body that has been attacked. It could have been anybody. How is this going to factor into the story?

"Just..." Moyer points to the door, "Stay here while I make sure that employee isn't going to be a problem."

Chapter 5

It's not as easy as you think. To really go through with it, you have to commit to the craft. You've got to go in with the act itself already premeditated. Giving Pendel the go-ahead, I was setting him up for failure.

Pendel wasn't going to cut into Hendrix's neck. No chance at all that he'd follow through, but sure, I watch from a sliver between the blinds. I watch how he pulls the knife on the editor, all those years shedding with every shiver. For that briefest of moments, I might have thought he could commit.

Because that's how this story's going to elevate me, and by me, I mean us, beyond anything that passes for breaking news. This story must resonate, and we're getting close. So close, in fact, I'm starting to feel it in my bones. Not one to be the anxious type, you could say I'm anticipatory. This is going really well. Too well?

When I say the words "I'll take care of it," he's already too far gone to put up a fight. It's a pact of sorts, Pendel distantly aware that oblivion is the only possible end. I become the lingering possibility, a last dash of hope, or not quite hope, exactly, but rather that final flicker of motivation for a character as the final act reaches its penultimate scene.

Pendel left with the body, I walk down that hallway, following his footsteps. From Pendel's end, we're facing an issue because he failed to commit. It's his fault, this failure that ruined what should have been another line in my body of work. I'm altogether pleased, willingly allowing him to sit in those wayward emotions, bask in the feeling of failure and rejection. Enjoy what it feels like to be an author, one of his clients.

The way things are, and the way things will come to pass... it's all part of the story. Frankly, I'm enjoying how the details have fallen into place almost effortlessly, just like I know Pendel won't be able to stay back for long. He'll come after me, too afraid to be by himself.

The employee hasn't gone very far.

The way this looks, it's bad. It's written to look bad.

Bloodcurdling screams coming from an office after-hours? For a young employee like this production assistant, it's nightmare fuel.

More reason to play around with the details, make a few edits on the fly. I had expected there to be interference; pain cannot be inflicted without a physical response. This young employee, I find him in one of the back rooms where large printers and other equipment rest. Spread out across the large table, acting as the focal point of space, are hundreds of galleys, early copies of a most-anticipated book release. The assistant must have been staying late to work on mailing lists. I can hear the fear in his voice as he speaks to someone over the phone.

"Yes, I know what I heard. Okay. Please hurry. I think he's hurt. Maybe a stroke!"

Security. It'll take them 10 minutes to arrive, but it'll only take five for me to step forward and for Pendel to spoil the story's impact yet again.

When the assistant is off the phone, I'll time it perfectly, rushing into the room, my panicked breaths muddying every word, my face blemished with Hendrix's blood.

"Oh my god," he says. He runs behind the table, unable to take in what he's seeing. "Oh my god, oh my god, oh my god..."

Don't piss yourself, kid.

I'm really playing it up, making use of every moment he and I have before this becomes predictably an escape, a final straw. Chewing the inside of my gums produces some additional blood splatter, enough that it discolors my teeth.

"You've got to help me!" I enjoy these sorts of details, the panic that comes with being so vulnerable, so near danger itself. It reminds you that you're alive. For a story to truly shine, you need these details. They give everyone who may live through it later a moment of pause, a glaring reminder that they are alive... but for how long? And who might be plotting their own twist, altering the trajectory of their story?

"Please, help me!" I start whimpering, letting the tears flow, and... yeah, why not? I trip and fall to my knees, taking a stack of galleys with me.

"Please, he's a monster. He wants me to... he..."

Enter an unaware Henry Richmond Pendel.

Watch as I change my tone, crawling forward, looking to get at the assistant, luring Pendel to chase after me. I lunge at the mortified assistant and whisper in his ears, "He made me do it. He makes his authors do it..."

Then it's Pendel grabbing me, and I'm playing it off like he wants me for dead. Could be a bit more effective, but the story registers, the assistant well-aware of the narrative possibilities. Hearing the elevator doors beeping, the assistant calls out, "Over here!"

There's our cue.

I crash into Pendel, "We need to move **now**." So unlike me to be afraid. It catches Pendel off-guard, resulting in him pulling me along with him as he breaks into a sprint. We navigate the halls, being spotted by at least one of the security guards as we take to the stairs. Two flights later, we're breaking a sweat as we make it to the sixth floor, finding an unoccupied closet to disappear into while security makes their rounds.

"What do we do now?" Pendel asks.

"What do you mean?" I say, flashing him a grin. "Things are going swimmingly. Imagine, they're in hot pursuit, and we're suddenly being placed into a sequence of events typically reserved for crime thrillers! We're in the thick of it, Pendel. We're in the thick of it and we're going to make sure nobody anticipates how it ends!"

Chapter 6

When Pendel's phone rings, they're still in hiding. Its ring echoes out like a siren call, directing those in pursuit to descend upon these two guilty criminals.

Moyer shakes his head, "You keep fucking up."

"I'm sorry," Pendel says, rushing to silence the phone. He ends the call, only to have yet another line up. "I'm really sorry."

"Apologies mean nothing if you keep repeating the same mistakes."

There is a palpable sense of urgency. Though they skirted by without being seen, it starts to become clear that they shouldn't have remained hidden in the closet for so long. The authorities have arrived. Moyer brings a finger to his lips. Pendel nods, cupping his mouth. Opening the door a crack, Moyer scans the hallway.

He looks up and down the hallway and then gives Pendel the go-ahead.

"Me first?" Pendel whispers.

Moyer remains stone cold, "How would you tell the story? Prove your worth."

This could be his last chance, Pendel realizes, and no, he isn't ready. Like the intended act of vengeance, fueled by betrayal,

Pendel can barely think straight; he's not going to win against the whirlpool of fear and feeling attacking him from within.

"Now," Moyer commands.

Pendel steps into the hallway, each footfall feeling heavy, his knees buckling and cracking as he proceeds down the hall. Listening for the authorities, he hears only the low hum of white noise, an office at rest. After a few steps, Pendel can breathe, focusing just enough on the task at hand. The sixth floor is clear, cushioning them to follow through on their departure.

"Stairs," Moyer whispers.

Looking over the railing to the floors below, another issue comes to mind: "The steps are steel. They are going to hear us."

Moyer pushes him down a flight of stairs.

Pendel collides with the landing below elbows-first, the steel grate tearing into his skin like a cheese grater. Moyer casually takes the steps, joining him as he struggles to his feet. "Any other questions?"

No. Their pace quickens from here. They make it to the second floor when they glimpse two outfits on the ground floor, likely alerted by their descent. Both Moyer and Pendel freeze mid-action, hiding under the thin veil of shadow cast across the second-floor landing.

Doesn't look good.

And then Pendel's phone rings again.

Voices from below ascend to signal to Moyer the severity of their situation.

"Failure, absolute failure," Moyer says.

The caller in question, it could be a familiar number, if Pendel had any ability to retain names or numbers. The call ends abruptly, replaced with a notification of a text message.

"Pick up the phone."

From here Moyer takes the lead. He grabs Pendel by the arm and pulls him into the hallway, quickly moving through the cafeteria Moyer grabs a few items from the kitchen, and they head for the elevator.

They duck inside.

Moyer hits the button for the top floor.

Pendel's phone rings three times and then drops.

"I said pick up the phone."

Moyer tries to grab at the device, but Pendel turns away, answering the call.

"You've got nowhere to run, asshole." He recognizes the voice. "We've found the body." Detective Monroe. "I could have given you the benefit of the doubt, Pendel, but you see, unlike you, I'm actually good at my job. I know my role. I'm here to represent justice... but you, you represent what's wrong with your fucking industry."

The elevator reaches the top floor, doors sliding open with a ding.

"Where are you going, Pendel?" The detective elongates his inquiry, confident in how the pursuit will conclude. "You're all out of options. Continuing to evade arrest will only worsen the circumstances that follow." Tonight, the detective believes the case will be closed. Yet there's still something in the shadows. Moyer presses the door close button and sends the elevator down. It's Moyer, and he knows how the story ends.

They take the elevator to the ground floor.

"We're waiting for you," says the detective.

Moyer listens in on the one-sided conversation, informing Pendel to remain silent—*don't put it on speaker.* Their next sequence will prove to be a challenge. Moyer is energized by the events, unable to keep from a wide grin forming ear to ear. When the elevator doors open, they won't be there. Rather, it'll be as Moyer planned: Taking to the darkness of the basement, following the cramped spaces and halls toward a back exit, a set of double doors reserved for large bulk shipments.

"Pendel, you're just delaying the inevitable," says Monroe.

Yet they've dodged police pursuit. In the alley between the office building and a nondescript warehouse, Moyer directs their next choice, beckoning for Pendel to search through the garbage bags, tearing into them and promptly removing the innards, while Moyer listens to the detective's threats, each new utterance acting more like a geolocator.

The garbage doesn't yield anything they can use, so Moyer

demonstrates what must be done as a plan B. They use the trash bags as clothing, the odor and grime caked between their skin and the suffocating plastic of the used bags.

"Find them!" The detective quickly loses sight of that confidence at the top of the call, taking it out on his subordinates.

Moyer continues to listen in on the call as they walk the avenue, block after block, becoming lost to the downward spiral of the night. People keep a wide distance, the would-be suspects having effectively donned the appearance of yet another showing of the city's homeless population.

"I'm going to find you, Pendel! You're fucking done!"

The call drops as they reach 14th Street. While waiting for the light to change, Moyer takes a breath and says, "We all have a story to tell..."

Pendel finishes his sentence, "...Some are willing to do anything to tell it."

Chapter 7

Oh, how he needs me. A story about him becomes a story about me. Eventually it'll be a story for the masses to examine and interpret, an entry point into a body of work that baffles and requires study and further understanding. He is clueless when caught off-guard, the foundation of life itself crumbles at his feet. Pendel has been reduced to a pupil, someone who needs my every instruction, especially now that the illusion of safety has been shattered.

We have only one objective, and that's to lengthen the time between now and our capture. So I'll take him back to where it started. It isn't safe to return to his apartment, yet it's safer to return to the hotel. It could be said that the killer often returns to the scene of the crime, motivations aplenty, likely to relive a memory from a previous act.

"Keep quiet and follow my every command."

He agrees. There'll be no more slip-ups. Pendel is an echo, and I'm the scream. We'll opt for the same room where I stayed. The smell of garbage lingers, but if you pay them enough under the table, anyone will look away.

Once we're in the room, he asks me, "How can you afford any of this?"

I peek out the window at the street below. "A death in the family opens doors."

This is where we will remain, in between the moment when they find us and the last hurrah. You could say we need one last workshop. You could say I need to get this last sequence right, so when I sit him down, it's as much a kill as it is a lesson.

"Listen to me," I say, his face in my hands. "We're not going to make it out of this. You must accept that we are both going to be arrested."

He nods, "I accept."

"Do you, though?"

"Yes," he says. For once, I believe him.

"Good," I say, inspecting the hotel room. "This was where I stayed, waiting for housekeeping to find Jerry's body. I couldn't sleep, you could say I was a mess of emotions. Everything was on the line. Now, in hindsight, that could be the formative moment in my entire career. It set the tone, and it taught me about patience. I learned by doing, and that in every act there is an opportunity to workshop a memory, a motivation, and finally, the misery of others." This is my last chance to reminisce, a chance to offer a retrospective. "Things could have easily fallen apart. Patience... yeah, I learned by doing. All those nights watching you. All that time learning the ins and outs of your authors. You could say I earned my MFA. A master of patience and pacing, the body of work I'm building, it's second to none. Really, think about it..."

He sits on the edge of the bed, listening to my every word.

"Are you thinking about the scale, the sheer magnitude of this story?"

Pendel has no idea, but it's good that he plays along, "Yeah. I am."

"Uh huh," I say, continuing the retrospective. I walk up to the far wall and press my palms against the surface. "I remember hearing the scream from behind this wall... the lone signal that it was all falling into place. You work on something for years, hoping that the story will add up, and when it finally does... there's just no replacement for that kind of rush. It's addictive, the essence of life itself. You feel me?"

He nods, "It's true."

I join him on the bed, sitting next to him. "What about you? What made you feel that rush, that feeling of being alive?"

Pendel's latest command: Reminisce, play along.

Naturally, he needs instruction, so I give him his prompt: "We're having our final moment before the big grandiose final scene. This is your chance to reminisce about your career, that moment when it first made sense."

"Oh," he says.

Still needs more instruction. Pendel's fading fast, the menace he had become no longer present. In its place, I see a broken man, a person stunted emotionally, lost to a sense of defeat and loneliness that I wouldn't wish on my worst enemy. On second thought...

"Okay fine, answer me this: What did you get out of seeing your authors compete for your attention?"

"Well," he exhales, "I think it was when Jerry, J.D. Church signed with me. He was already an established author. By then I had too many clients, too many authors, but I needed to earn enough to stay afloat."

"I see. Keep going."

He doesn't notice that I'm recording our entire conversation.

"Jerry sold well, and his deals were easy. I saw in him this hunger for validation that sort of... I don't know... jostled free an understanding of just how fragile and sensitive authors are. When I saw the very same Jerry fall apart when faced with a bad review of his latest book, I think I figured out how to psychologically manipulate an author into always feeling that high of validation. When they didn't meet my mark, I'd ice them out, make them feel like nothing, which would cause them to work even harder." He stalls on a thought, "...anyway, yeah they all started to fight for my attention, and I loved how it made me feel."

I end the recording and stand up from the bed, "Well..." Back to the window, the street below, spotting the vehicle, our ride to the final scene. "You're about to get one more opportunity to feel."

"What, umm?"

Grabbing his arm, I offer his latest instruction: "We're going on a trip."

"But they're looking for us..."

I nod, "Yeah, and they're going to find us in the bright lights, right in the open, for all to see and discuss!"

Pendel can remain in the dark, unwilling to see the full picture. Our little retrospective ends with more evidence and an inclination of how I see this story ending. Though he might be catching up, I leave a few details out, just in case Pendel needs an extra push when it comes time to deliver.

"The car's waiting outside," I say. "We don't want to be late!"

Better to go out in a blaze than be lost to the silence after the last sentence.

CHAPTER 8

Author of MURK and the acclaimed MY TIME IN THE HEARTLAND **Mallory McAllister's THE NOT SO ENDLESS NIGHT**, an examination of masculinity under the guise of serial killers and their upbringing, to **Gretchen Olsteen** at **Hachette**, in a significant deal, for publication in fall 20█, by **Erin Gossamer** at **Wiley.**

Pendel sees the deal announcement on the ride to the airport. By the time they make it on the plane, the cops have swarmed the terminal. Lucky, one could say, in that both make it off the tarmac, into the sky, well on their way to the planned demise. Moyer keeps him in the dark, though Pendel is beginning to solve the puzzle. If the story must end tragically, he assumes that Moyer will take his life. Eventually, the same blade that has tasted many an author's blood will spill his own across the carpet, leaving behind a scene that will be celebrated by some and studied by others. This is Pendel's only hope, the story yielding his own death.

Moyer falls asleep next to him, the flight lulling Pendel into a temporary sense of relief. They are just two passengers on their way to a conference.

That's where they are going, Pendel assumes. From the ticket, it's written plainly, Eastern Iowa Airport (CID). Cedar Rapids. Pendel has been there before. The Iowa Writers Workshop. It's about that time for the weeklong Mission Creek festival. Somewhere between all the events, there could be an obligation, programming with Pendel's name on it.

The ticket is the final piece. Moyer is taking them to the epicenter, where authors both established and emerging gather. Led to the slaughter. Being led to the slaughter.

Pendel's life does not flash before his eyes.

Rather, he enjoys a would-be tender moment with a retrospective, a real one, the one he wouldn't share with Moyer, or anybody else. He uses his phone and scrolls through all the screencaps and photos he has saved. Shuffled through miscellaneous photos and memes are those moments, the real moments, when he felt appreciated and grateful, the moments when he saw all his work produce a positive effect.

He stops on an image, the acknowledgements page of a book by an author, one of his authors, the name now eluding him. A shame, one that produces a flicker of guilt and embarrassment before he reads those lines, the reason for taking the photo in the first place. "To my agent and true believer, Henry Richmond Pendel. You're a rock star, and thank you for fighting the good fight. This book wouldn't exist without your courage."

His courage.

Don't know about that...

Pendel swipes, the image replaced with another. It's an author interview, again the name of this author, his author, missing from his memory. Yet there it is, more evidence of him being a good person: "So many years of just sucking at writing. That's what you'll have to do if you want to get good at anything. You got to suck before you can blow... people away. Anyway, I didn't have much left in the tank, so to speak. I was querying agents and wrote something like eight novels before I ever heard back from anyone that wasn't an instant pass. One day I'm ready to quit and the next,

I get an email from an agent, and not just any agent: It's, yeah, Henry Pendel! That's all it took, seeing him respond to my writing. He asked to send the full MS. Like a week later I had representation. Pendel sent the manuscript to some editors and fast forward like a month later and I became a published author."

Maybe not a good person, but at least a good agent.

Another image, this one is a photo of Pendel and Mal. She's so happy in this photo. He has his arm around her, Mal grinning widely. Where was this? Pendel squints, glimpsing what was captured in the background of the photo. Then it hits him suddenly.

"Ah!"

Moyer shifts in his seat.

Pendel holds his breath, waiting for Moyer to settle.

This was the book launch, after party. She had just launched her debut at The Strand. *My Time in the Heartland* was getting a lot of attention. He even looks happy in the photo. This was before things fell apart. The future looked bright.

Pendel sighs, swiping to the next capture.

Why did he save this one?

It's a headline: LITERATURE IS NOT THE SAME AS PUBLISHING, most of the article cut off. It looks to be about an independent publisher, Coffee House Press, with nothing to do with him. Still, Pendel rereads the headline, reflecting on this image. When it clicks, he remembers that he had been on the board of directors, made a sizeable donation. Back then he had the right motivations. He wasn't yet making donations simply for tax purposes or to get that public nod. He took this screencap because it was back when he believed that a book could be more than its pages, a story more than its tale. Elevating the life on the page, elevating the authors who made their sacrifice to produce a manuscript.

He can't stand it, swiping to another image.

This one's a video, and before he can lower the volume or better yet delete it, the brunt of its message hits him hard. There he is, Jerry on Letterman, peak of his career, *Harvest Falls* had just come out, and he's chatting about Pendel.

"He talked me off the ledge," says Jerry.

Letterman sets him up to tell a heartfelt tale of an author and his agent, an author facing the biggest lesson of his career and how his agent helped him fight, when all he wanted to do was end his own life. Pendel knows the truth. The way Jerry lies, it's so convincing.

He must be an author, and a damn good one.

None of it is true. And of course, it was done to make Jerry seem infallible, a weak hero, one that people can relate to, at a time when both Pendel and Jerry were afraid that one of his students was going to press charges.

Pendel replays the video. By the time he goes for a third viewing, the tenderness of his retrospective is shattered, wiped clean and replaced with the punishing shame and fear that will consume his final day of freedom.

Chapter 9

When we get to the campus, the festival is in full swing. Looks like they aren't familiar with his or my story, which is unexpected. We're greeted by a student named Iain, who is excited to be on the so-called "welcome committee." He finds us as we're walking around the tiny little downtown area, seeing that many a writer has already begun taking advantage of the festivities.

"It's a fun weekend," says Iain. "Boozy and bookish."

I'll take the lead, having briefed Pendel on the plane ride to Cedar Rapids to remain silent. As always, he must follow me, not the other way around. He wears fear so well, it'll be up to me to make it a costume, one that keeps all these emerging authors, these hopeful and ambitious writers, believing in the reputation long enough for our final scene.

Back in the city, he's a bust, reputation death, yet here, they seem to be oblivious. Could it be that they still hope for a breakthrough? Across social media, Pendel has been discussed as an agent of toxicity, with many agents offering their own criticisms of how he conducted business. Editors denounce their relationships with Pendel. Authors remain divided: Some still seeing him as a potential agent acceptance while others, typically the more knowledgeable of the industry dealings, know that even if one were to sign with Pendel now, he wouldn't be able to get an editor to answer his emails or calls.

"Looks like people aren't wasting a single moment to pregame," I say, noticing a group of students openly imbibing from tallboys.

Iain laughs, "You know how it is."

I do.

"Work hard, play hard," I say.

The point here is to relate, to become like the students, an author hopeful for a breakthrough. Where victim could become equally villain, it all depends on how the story unfolds, and I'm already three steps ahead. It'll be in that workshop. There I will be, and so will Pendel, apprehended and caught in the act.

"We can come back later, but you guys kind of arrived a little late and we're short on time," Iain says. "Let me show you where housing and your rooms are, so you can drop off what you need."

"Naw," I say. "We're good."

A look cast in Pendel's direction, he isn't paying attention, a contemplative gaze cast across the idyllic campus scene, the same one that I have paid barely any attention.

"Well good," Iain says, grinning widely. "Was cutting it short but this changes things!"

"Then we can be early," I say.

Turns out Iain is in the workshop. Outside the classroom, he tells me the situation, "So this is the advanced fiction workshop, but it's a small crew today, six, seven including me. You're his handler, right?"

I jab Pendel with my finger, getting his attention.

"Oh, no. No. I'm just along for the ride."

"Oh," Iain says. "Okay. I just assumed..." Changing the subject, he asks me if I'm a writer. To which yes, I'll reciprocate. Better yet, I'll even go so far as to show a little vulnerability, "I am, or at least trying to. It's been grueling out there. I think everyone's burnt out." That's enough to make me amiable to an ambitious student and writer like Iain, who not only understands my situation but also secretly believes he won't arrive at the same fate, not when he's attending such a prestigious MFA program like the Iowa

Writers Workshop. Instant doors opened to possible agent representation and book deals.

Pendel's turn to say something: "Glad to be here."

"We're all excited," says Iain. "Do you need anything before we get started? We got water and access to a projector, should you require it."

He gives me a look, yet again going against my command.

"I'm fine," he says. "Thank you."

"Well okay," Iain grins. "I'll head inside and intro you in a few minutes."

"Sure thing," I say, implying that we will follow him into the classroom shortly.

Iain has his hand on the doorknob, "Oh, yes. Right." He gestures in the direction of the room, "We'll all get situated then."

"Great," I say. "Thanks!"

When he's gone, I pull Pendel in close. "You can't fuck this up. This is it, the final scene. We're not making it past this point."

He sighs, "I know."

"Don't make eye contact," I tell him. "You're going to want to stick to what I've told you, keep to the discussion points."

"Okay," he says.

"And here," I hand him a knife.

He hesitates, "I don't think I can..."

"Don't you worry, I'm here to help." I show him that I've got my own blade tucked away in my handy bag.

A workshop professor passes us in the hallway, instantly recognizing Pendel. She stops, turns around, and walks the way she arrived.

"Everybody recognizes me," he says.

"Isn't that what you want?"

I go in first, finding a seat up front. Give the students around me a little greeting. Just the usual hey and to the lone student who seemed a bit curious about my appearance, a curt explanation, "They said I could audit the class so..."

The door opens, a grand entrance.

Henry Richmond Pendel.

He can still turn it on when he wants to, huh?

I'm impressed. He takes his position at the front of the classroom, Iain quickly giving a gushy introduction, one that would be heartfelt and kind if it wasn't so obviously made in hopes of a later offer to query and to be considered as a client.

Pendel grins, "Thanks, Iain, for such a warm welcome. I have to say, I always look forward to a visit to the Iowa Writers Workshop. I know I'm getting the best in every regard: The best accommodations, the best conversations, and the best, most talented writers. I always joke with my colleagues, saying that when you visit Iowa Writers, what you're really doing is going shopping."

He gets a minor pop, laughter from the cohort of students.

"It's kind of true," he says. I notice the lowering of his right hand, reaching for the weapon stowed away and hidden behind his back. He exhales, "I'd love to quickly go around the room, have each of you tell me your name, your track—fiction, nonfiction, poetry—and your goals, yes that's the big question, goals as an author. Do you want to become a bestselling author? Do you want to eventually work in the film industry? Do you want to write the Great American Novel? Sky's the limit."

Everyone remains silent.

A student in the back says, "Isn't that kind of, like, presumptuous?"

Pendel frowns, "We're all being open and honest here. That's what a workshop is for, isn't it?"

"I guess," says another student.

It's my cue to speak up, "I want to be remembered."

That gets everybody's attention, and Pendel, he finally keeps up his end of the story, that recognizable glut of confidence when he says, "You'll have to be willing to do anything..."

"To tell your story," I say, finishing his sentence.

What follows is a final exhale, pure violence to preempt the consequences of our actions.

Chapter 10

There are seven students, seven victims, all willing participants in the final scene of a most distressing kind of story. Pendel glimpses the inner wants and desires of each emerging author:

"I want to be a full-time author."

"I want to win the National Book Award."

"I want to see my books turned into films."

"I want to be an acclaimed author and professor."

"I... just want to be famous. Like David Foster Wallace."

"I want people to read my stuff long after I'm dead."

And the last student, Mr. Welcome Committee, Iain, expresses his own desire, "I just want my parents to be proud of me."

Moyer's willingness to be so open about his desire causes the rest of the workshop to lower their guard. Pendel congratulates everyone on their candor, their honesty, and proceeds to explain the publishing industry, how it's more than a well-written story, much more than quality and charisma. "It's about who you know," he says, "and who you're willing to connect with."

He discusses different networking strategies, including being a literary citizen to a community of authors to get your name out, starting your own journal or indie press, and even going so far as to move to a city with a big scene and play the socialite card.

The cohort listens intently, Pendel expertly worldbuilding while Moyer becomes just another author in the workshop.

"I think now's a good time to..." From its sheath, Pendel reveals the knife. "Make a few edits. Who would like to go first?"

The cohort is indifferent to the reveal of the weapon, remaining in their seats, holding their works-in-progress close, perhaps expecting the brandishing of a knife to be some metaphor for the grueling nature of writing and rejection.

A voice speaks up, Moyer's hand raised, "I'll go."

Pendel doesn't know what's happening. He's followed the script, yet when Moyer volunteers, he effectively derails his next move. Pendel was supposed to pick on a student, forcing them to offer their work, and from there, they'd discuss it as one would in a workshop, except whenever Pendel found something ill-fitting, he was to physically hurt the student.

Moyer's choice to be the first changes everything. Joining him at the front of the room, Pendel does his best to maintain composure, "Great, it's so great when we have a daring and fearless volunteer!" Yet between actions, Pendel tries to communicate with Moyer.

In a hushed whisper, Pendel asks Moyer for new commands.

When he holds the knife above his head, Pendel asks, "Am I supposed to kill you?"

The knife as a weapon and metaphor becomes the focal point of the presentation. Moyer doesn't give Pendel anything, instead defaulting with, "Follow my lead."

"Okay, so you're a novelist then?" Pendel's reaching, blind to what's about to happen.

"I am," says Moyer. "Aspiring novelist." He chuckles, "I didn't get into Iowa Writers but I'm here for Mission Creek, so I figured, why not sit in on this, this really important lecture?"

"Right," says Pendel. "Thank you for your interest. It always makes a person feel great knowing that people fought to hear them speak."

Moyer tells the class, "I think I'm just desperate, you know? I'll do anything to be published."

"Anything huh?"

Moyer issues the latest command, "Now. Knife. My shoulder."

"No way," says Pendel.

"Do it," says Moyer.

"It doesn't make any sense to..."

"I said do it!" Moyer grabs his free arm, "You're going to stab me because you want to be remembered. You'll stab me because there isn't a better way to end the story."

What this looks like to the students: Pendel and Moyer inches from each other, backs turned to the classroom. They get every third or fourth word, and then there's still the recognition of a weapon and a volunteer. This doesn't add up, not in a workshop environment.

One of the students speaks up, "I'm having trouble following, umm..."

"Now," Moyer hisses. "Now!"

Put on the spot, the pressures of everything that preceded this scene, the story completes its circle with an inceptive stab, the blade cutting into Moyer's left shoulder.

The pain is possibly enough, yet Moyer sells it well, instantly in tears, crawling toward a now quite stunned group of students.

Pendel loses sight of himself, the feelings bottled up coming out in a rage. "I didn't mean to hurt the guy! He did it to himself!"

The students don't believe him, "We saw you. You stabbed him!"

"Yeah," says another. "We saw it all!"

Moyer holds onto his left arm, "Please don't do this."

"I'm not going to do anything," Pendel says.

"Someone, get someone!"

Pendel points at a fallen Moyer, "He told me to stab him!"

"No, please," Moyer begs. "Please, someone, stop him please!"

It'll be Iain that steps forward, coming to the rescue, and it'll be like a flinch, Pendel at peak pressure and stress, being publicly prosecuted for a command, the latest in a long line of manipulation. Iain rushes forward and gets a blade in the neck. Nobody sees that coming, not even Moyer. What follows is more violence, a friend of Iain clamoring over his dying body, and then attempting an attack on Pendel, who is too far gone, operating on sheer anger and panic, to prevent additional attacks.

He slashes at one student's stomach, cutting through their shirt and stomach, deep enough to offer a peek at their innards. Another student loses an ear. The student that attempts an escape gets perhaps the worst that Pendel has to offer, not one but five stabs in the back.

"Please..."

Moyer watches from the floor, on his knees, one hand over his face, the other pressed against the stab wound. He flashes a grin, full recognition of the story being complete.

Pendel is out of breath, dropping the knife. His entire body is coated in a layer of red, eyes wide on a classroom full of menacing details. It clicks, understanding what just happened. Pendel doesn't feel anything, not anymore. Never again.

He leaves the front of the room, stepping over a body or two to get to a seat in the back. He joins the lone student in her seat, clenched into a ball, mortally afraid.

She whimpers.

What else can be said? Pendel catches his breath. Eventually, he turns to the student and asks her, "Did that really happen, or did I just imagine it?"

Pendel's cell phone rings, a number familiar, a name forgotten until he accepts the call.

"Put the knife down, Pendel."

Detective Monroe. Right on time.

Chapter 11

They'll find me on the ground with the other authors, victims of a collective fear. Detective Monroe spares nothing, bringing in enough units to swarm the perimeter of the building and surrounding campus, effectively derailing the festivities, the new and unexpected main event being the capture of Henry Richmond Pendel. *(And an emerging author named Alexander Moyer.)* That's okay, it's all according to the story and how it needs to be told. All part of revision and ensuring the best possible ending.

It doesn't take any longer than a half hour to deflate the scene, the authorities securing every room and hallway until they find Pendel bloodied at the front of the room.

He doesn't put up a fight. When the detective storms into the room, heading right for Pendel, his reaction is telling of the events to unfold.

"I can explain!"

Monroe grabs him and shoves him face-first against the wall, cuffing the man without saying a word. No Miranda Rights, nothing. He is dragged out of the room while three other outfits tend to the varying states of the victims.

I'm face up on the ground, the wound in my shoulder enough to play off while I wait until they get to me.

"Where were you stabbed?"

I release my grip on the wound, showing them the worst of it. "Shoulder."

"Just the shoulder?"

I nod.

In an instant, it seems, the room is crowded, arms reaching, and bodies being lifted onto stretchers, but maybe it's the relief, or maybe it's the pain because I'm finding it difficult to focus. The sequence of events blurs together, and I'm unable to think or speak clearly until much later, when I'm sitting up on a stretcher, my wound dressed, and there he is, Detective Monroe, sauntering up to me because he must know more than he's letting on.

I've prepared for this moment. He'll expect a confession, factoring me into Pendel's downfall; he'll expect that I am an accomplice, when I'll soon reveal to him that I am innocent, a young author manipulated by a man who has made a career out of using others.

"Alex?"

I ball my hand into a fist, "Yeah?" I unclench my hand, getting the blood flow going, the nerves in my arm remain tense, sending signals that cause jolts of pain. Pendel didn't get me clean. "That's me." I try to shake it off, annoyed that he couldn't get any of it right.

"I'm Detective Monroe," he says, like I don't already know.

"Hi," I say, remaining distant. Remember—I'm supposed to be traumatized by the events. I'm supposed to be in a lot of pain, not just physical. When he looks at me, he must see a person that will never again be the same. Something like this changes a person.

"How are you feeling?"

The look I give him says everything.

"Yeah, I know," he says, looking at his phone. "Mind if I ask you a few questions?" He eyes one of the paramedics standing near my stretcher. "I realize this might not be a good time, but, well, can we begin?"

Not about to ease off the tears. Instead, I nod and start sobbing loudly, "Just ask them."

He sighs, "This is difficult for you, I know... how do you know Henry Pendel?"

"He..." This is it, the best part. Allow me to manipulate you, Detective Monroe. "He said I was his author."

"His author?" Of course, he won't understand.

"Yeah, he owned me," I say. "And..."

"So he was your literary agent?"

Slow nod. "Yeah."

"I see," he says, typing out a note. "One Kevin Armisen, a production assistant at Alfred A. Wolf, said in our interview, I quote, 'He begged me for help. I was too afraid to do anything. He said he was making him do things.' Care to explain?"

"He made me..." I choke up. Let the tears flow. Be the image of a psychologically manipulated individual. He'll see how I fall apart, and it'll make him feel bad.

"I hate that I have to ask you this, but... were you there when he murdered Jeremiah Church?"

I nod slowly, "I was there for all of it."

He shakes his head, "My god. Can you explain further? What did he make you do?"

Hello full confession, complete with a nervous breakdown. "He told me... I had to prove myself... and, and..." Time for a visual aid, tearing the bandages off my stab wound, "He threatened to hurt me and make sure my career was over if I didn't meet his benchmarks."

"Benchmarks?"

"It was them or me," I say. "I had to kill to have Pendel all for myself."

Stunned, the detective calls for another to join him, yet he is distracted when I begin tearing at those fresh stitches. "Hey," he raises a hand. "Don't do that."

I'm not going to stop.

He's not going to stop me.

The blood will flow.

The rumors will circulate.

I'm going to do some *hard time*.

No escaping a sentence.

35 years in prison, something about being an accessory, after seven years there'll be an opportunity for parole. During the uproar, there'll be fascination mounting in the media. They'll see him as the menace he always was, amplified into an example of a human monster. Me, I'll become Alexander Moyer, the author who went through hell and back. Some will hate, others will hope for healing. Inevitably, it will be as I had thought all along, hiccups and all:

I will become infamous, both in name and the body of work accumulated over so many kills. Infamy transcends, becoming a source of financial gain and the foundation for my career to follow. This will become fact long after the fiction fades away. A story will take time to be fully told, but the pieces, I can rest in my cell peacefully knowing that they are all in place.

He doesn't ask me why, why Pendel did this to me, to his clients, and finally to himself. So it's up to me to tell him before I am restrained and later cuffed. Just like any story worth telling, you got to risk it all. What I tell him becomes the last sentence of the story.

"We all have a story to tell; some are willing to do anything to tell it."

Emily,

What a wonderful lunch yesterday! I'm still buzzing over what you said about him. How insane is that?! I want nothing more than for us to work together on finding you the best manuscripts and the authors most befitting of your talents and taste. I aspire to be nothing like my former employer, who shall not be named. I've put in a lot of hard work building new professional relationships with editors, and I'm actively building my list. In fact, I have one such author that I think you'd dig. It just might be a perfect fit. You'll recognize the name because there have already been so many articles and features about him. There was also that documentary about him. You know the name, Alexander Moyer. There's already been interest from other publishers, but I have yet to go out on submission. I've been waiting for the right pairing, and I think you and Alex might just hit it off. The way I see it, this could be the beginning of a long career for all three of us! As his agent, I'll do anything for him. An agent looks out for their authors, just like an editor wants the best of an author's words.

Let me know if you're interested in having a look, and I'll send over his memoir (yes! A MEMOIR!!)!

Sincerely,

Marina Grace
Literary Agent
Cooper Willis Endeavor

Deal of the Day

Author **Alexander Moyer**'s memoir, **MY AGENT, MY AUTHOR**, an exploration of his capture by controversial literary agent Henry Richmond Pendel and the murderous events that unfolded; **TO MANDATE HEAVEN**, the untold stories and traumas of the author's nomadic childhood and volatile adolescence; and **FRIENDS SELLING FRIENDS**, a debut novel about a group of twentysomethings in a heated game of wit and violence as wagers are increasingly dangerous and no one's life is off limits, to **Emily Mills** at **FSG**, in a seven-figure deal, by **Marina Grace** at **Cooper Willis Endeavor** (US).

About the Author

MICHAEL J. SEIDLINGER is the Filipino-American author of *Anybody Home?*, *The Body Harvest,* and other books. He has written for, among others, *Wired, Buzzfeed, Polygon,* and *Publishers Weekly*. You can find him at michaeljseidlinger.com.

Also by Michael J. Seidlinger

THE BODY HARVEST

ANYBODY HOME?

MY PET SERIAL KILLER

SCREAM (OBJECT LESSONS)

MARK Z. DANIELEWSKI'S HOUSE OF LEAVES: BOOKMARKED

Also by CLASH Books

THE BODY HARVEST

Michael J. Seidlinger

ANYBODY HOME?

Michael J. Seidlinger

INVAGINIES

Joe Koch

LETTERS TO THE PURPLE SATIN KILLER

Joshua Chaplinsky

EVERYTHING THE DARKNESS EATS

Eric LaRocca

VIOLENT FACULTIES

Charlene Elsby

CHARCOAL

Garrett Cook

THE MIDNIGHT MUSE

Jo Kaplan

I CAN FIX HER

Rae Wilde

OF BEASTS

M. Jane Worma

www.ingramcontent.com/pod-product-compliance
Lightning Source LLC
Jackson TN
JSHW022333300825
90255JS00003B/4
9781960988812